FALLING FOR THE CHIEFTON
Enchanted Falls, Book 3
Copyright © 2018 by Keira Montclair

This is a work of fiction. Names, characters, places and incidents are either the product of the author's imagination or are used fictitiously, and any resemblance to actual persons, living or dead, business establishments, events or locales is entirely coincidental.

Printed in the USA.

Cover Design and Interior Format
© THE KILLION GROUP, INC.

ENCHANTED FALLS

BOOK
3

FALLING
for the
CHIEFTAIN

A TIME TRAVEL ROMANCE

KEIRA
MONTCLAIR

NOVELS BY

KEIRA MONTCLAIR

CHAPTER ONE

The Highlands of Scotland

ALLISON SUTTON'S FEET HIT WATER as she plunged into the murky liquid at the base of the cascading falls. Holding back a scream, she fought her way to the top of the pool, kicking her feet as hard as she could and doing the breaststroke to speed her ascension. The pool was surprisingly warm, almost bubbling with an energy all its own. She should have known this would be special.

When she finally made it to the surface, she broke into a huge grin. Caroline may have been the one to insist the Sutton sisters end their trip to the Highlands by jumping from the Highland waterfall, but she was proud of herself—of all of them—for actually going through with it.

"Hannah, that was the best!"

She didn't see either of her sisters, so she spun in a circle as she treaded water, waiting for them to rise to the top. "Caroline? I'm so glad we did this. Where the hell are you?"

Silence.

She twirled around in another circle, looking for any sign of her sisters.

Nothing.

She fought a sudden surge of panic. She'd always been the weakest swimmer—if she'd made it to the top, her sisters must have, too. Maybe they were playing a trick on her…

She swam to the edge, surprised to find a huge rock she'd not noticed before. In fact, the whole pool was surrounded by rocks. She crept out, an eerie feeling shooting from her toes up to her head. Something was different. This was not the area she'd stared down at before jumping.

Peering up at the top of the waterfall, she gaped in disbelief. It wasn't there. There was no cascading water, no sound of water hitting the pool beneath it. Instead, an eerie, unnerving quiet hung in the air.

She whirled around, shaking water off her body to ease the chill, and squeezed her sopping wet hair. Not knowing what else to do, she walked around the area, tugging her ponytail out of habit.

The more she moved, the more her panic escalated.

The waterfall was gone. Simply gone. And so were her sisters.

How the hell had this happened?

Maybe this was a dream—the faulty logic of the jump felt like dream logic—but her wet clothes clung to her skin and she could reach down and touch the rocks surrounding the pool. Everything *felt* real. Either way, sitting here shivering wouldn't do her any good. If it was a dream, she'd awaken soon, and if it wasn't? She needed to find someone with a cell phone so she could call her sisters. Maybe she'd hit her head and lost a few hours.

She was a registered nurse—she'd seen stranger things happen.

Trying to shake off the panicky feeling, she walked away from the pond. Surely, she'd find someone soon.

Except she didn't. There was no sign of civilization anywhere. The farther Allie walked, the denser the vegetation around her. About half an hour later, she managed to locate a path, so she took a deep breath and chose a direction.

She'd have to meet someone eventually.

Breannainn MacKay picked the bastard up, hefted him over his shoulder, and tossed him over the roped area with a roar.

"Yay, Brann!" his wee brother Lachie yelled. "Ye did it! Ye beat another."

Brann couldn't help but smile as he leaned over to catch his breath, watching his subdued opponent toss a bag of coin to the man who'd taken the wagers. He then limped away, cursing all the while.

Brann knew few of the men in the audience had wagered against him. They knew better.

The onlookers cheered as he moved over to his wee brother, who held out a skin of water. He took several swigs, then poured the rest over the top of his head, swinging his long dark hair back and forth to cool himself down.

And perhaps to instigate the crowd with a bit of

show.

"Black Brann! Black Brann! Black Brann!" they roared.

He finally turned to look at the crowd of over a hundred men who'd come to watch him wrestle. He did his best to build his reputation as the fiercest warrior in the Highlands. Some days he fought with his sword, some days with his fists. His smile broadened as he stared at the crowd going berserk over his prowess.

Becoming champion of all the Highlands was his new goal in life.

But then his gaze found the one person he hadn't wanted to see. His middle brother, Taran, stood at the back of the crowd. He didn't chant or applaud but watched the proceedings with a sadness in his gaze.

Well, Taran had chosen his path. Let him reap the consequences.

Brann had been betrothed to Shona MacDonnell, but she'd fallen in love with Taran. They'd married less than a year ago, making Brann MacKay the laughingstock of the Highlands.

He'd vowed to beat every last fool who dared to ridicule him, and he was pleased that he'd nearly met his goal. No one had insulted him to his face for many moons, though occasionally an overconfident lad would still face him. The matches were held on the corners—a stretch of land between Brann's land and three neighboring properties: Murray, Sinclair, and MacDonnell. They all benefited from having a place for clan members to sell their wares, and they split a portion of the wagers made on the matches or contests held there.

Proving his prowess in these matches might improve his mood, but he held a grudge against his brother. As far as he was concerned, Taran was dead to him. Unfortunately, they were still linked by the only family member they had left—Lachie. Their wee brother had no mother or father to guide him, so it was Brann's job to raise him. He had promised his mother to watch over the youngest of the three brothers when she'd passed on from fever six years ago. Lachie was now only eight summers, and Brann knew better than to ask one who was so young to choose between his brothers. He wished to teach the lad to think for himself, so he allowed him to make his own choices and did not hold those choices against him. Lachie's choice was to love them both.

"Brann, Taran is here. See? He's in the back. Shall we go speak with him? For certes, he'll congratulate ye." Lachie's eyes shone with the same gleam of hope that had been there for a year now. The lad's persistence hadn't wavered one bit. Brann couldn't fault him for it.

"Nay, Lachie. I'll nae speak with him, and ye know it."

Lachie came up to him and whispered as the crowd dispersed, "Ye know ye dinnae love her. Why can ye nae be friendly? Please, Brann? I love Taran and Shona. She's carrying. They could have a niece or nephew for ye to love."

True, he hadn't loved Shona, but they'd been betrothed for two years. His sire had made the arrangement, wanting to ensure his line bore heirs, before passing away from a bad wound.

Shona MacDonnell was everything a wife should

be: beautiful, kind, compassionate. She'd not stirred Brann at all, but even so…Taran had paid him, and their father, the ultimate insult by breaking the betrothal, and such a thing could not easily be forgotten or forgiven.

Brann took a strip of his plaid and wiped the sweat from his face. "Nay, Lachie. If ye wish to speak with him, then go on with ye. I'll no' care."

"But why, Brann?" The laddie gazed up at him with such admiration and innocence that he hated to disappoint him.

"Because 'tis my heir Shona should be carrying. Go on with ye, now." He took another swig of water and waved his brother off.

A loud shriek rent the air, so he turned to seek out the source. There was some kind of melee at the far end of the clearing, though too many onlookers had gathered about for him to see anything.

Another scream echoed through the open space, too high-pitched to be from a man. His brow furrowed. Women were allowed only for the fairs and festivals. The men knew better than to bring their womenfolk to tourneys and battles. There should not be a lass here at all.

He strode toward the melee, which was becoming louder by the minute, and watched as more of the crowd did the same.

When he reached the edge of the group, he peered over the heads of the gathered men, surprised to see a head of golden hair in the middle. The lass kicked any man who came too near, sending some of them flying. Her shining hair was pulled back and bounced in the air with every one of her moves.

None of the men appeared to be harming her, but the sight of a lone lass standing in the middle of over fifty men did not settle well. His father's words rang out to him. *A lass does no' have the muscle of a lad. By your honor as a Highlander, never raise your hand to someone who cannae fight back.*

His sire had also pledged to haunt him if he ever allowed one of his brothers—or indeed, any of his clanmates—to hit a woman. As laird of his keep, it was his job to protect the innocent, even if they were not of his clan.

Brann's bellow stopped the men short as he forced his way into the crowd, pushing and shoving at four different plaids, until he reached the center and stood face to face with the lass.

She froze as the crowd parted, panting as if she'd been battling for hours. He'd expected to see a lass in tears, but instead her face held a fury he hadn't seen in many of his opponents.

She shouted something at him in a strange tongue or twist of an accent, but her stance told him exactly what she wanted. *Stay away.*

Rather than comply with her wishes, Black Brann advanced toward her. There was only one reason he moved forward—the woman was gorgeous— and her golden hair and blue eyes beckoned him. He knew it was foolish, especially since he'd seen her kick as high as a man's head with those long, lithe legs, but he was powerless to stop himself. It was as if he was drawn to her by some mysterious source.

She shouted again at him, and when he didn't stop, she bent over at the waist, leaning away from him, and kicked him square in his bollocks.

He'd been quick enough to catch her oddly covered foot before she connected with all her strength. Her force and aim had been greatly diminished by his arm, but she'd connected with her target enough for him to nearly drop to his knees.

A hush covered the crowd in an instant.

Black Brann, champion of the Highlands, had just been bested by a lass.

CHAPTER TWO

ALLIE GULPED AS SHE HIT her target. Of all the men she'd squared off with, why had she chosen to hit the tallest and most muscular one in the balls? It would probably only piss him off.

She'd been crazy to stroll into a clearing full of men, especially men dressed so oddly, and think she'd find one who'd help her. They had the biggest swords she'd ever seen strapped to their bodies, and their clothing appeared to be from ancient times.

A phone. All she needed was a phone. Yes, she was in a foreign country, but surely Scots carried phones. Even ones who dressed like they were attending a medieval festival and acted like cavemen.

What kind of group was this, anyway? Was she about to be sacrificed to a cult god, or were they just fools who didn't bathe?

A queasiness deep in her belly insisted something deeply strange was going on here—stranger even than being circled by a group of big, burly, badly dressed men—but she didn't have time to dwell on it. The fury on the face of the man in front of her called her back to her present circumstance. She knew how painful it was for a man to take a blow to his testicles. She'd even suffered a ruptured cyst on her ovaries, and one of her textbooks had said the pain was comparable. Both organs were well protected because of their reproductive purpose for the species. Her nurse's training never left her, but something told her the man in front of her, struggling to speak from her kick, wouldn't care for an anatomy lesson.

"I warned you. I warned all of them." She swept her arm around in a semicircle. Her words rang out in the clearing, the hush that her blow had caused louder than any shouting she'd ever heard before. "Yet you continued to move. None of you have the right to touch me, so keep your distance."

The tic in the man's jaw told her he still struggled, but his gaze never left hers as he forced himself to a standing position. Every male face in the area stared at them, no doubt waiting to see how he would retaliate.

The whispers began in an odd dialect she couldn't quite understand. Some of it was close to the Scottish brogue she'd heard since she and her sisters had arrived in Scotland, but others were totally unintelligible. The ones she could make out were not the kind of words she'd hoped to hear.

She was about to die.

"Black Brann is going to kill the wench."

"Who would dare hit Black Brann?"

"She's a dead woman."

"Her words are odd. I thought her English, but

nay. Those arenae English words."

"If she be English, he'll kill her for certes."

"She's nae English. Look at the wench, would ye?"

"How do ye think he'll kill her, slowly or so fast she'll no' see it coming?"

"I wager slow!"

She heard the group place their wagers on her possible murder, but she stood her ground. Allison Sutton, all five foot six of her, stood there in her wet skinny jeans, her peasant top clinging to her average-sized breasts, and stared down the huge Highlander standing in front of her. Maybe she should explain that she'd learned to kick that way thanks to her countless ballet classes.

Again, he didn't look like he would care.

In fact, he looked as though he'd strolled off the pages of one of Jennae Vale's Thistle and Hive Series novels. Her characters had traveled across a bridge and ended up in a different century.

That twist in her gut became painful. The heroines of those books had time traveled to ancient Scotland. These brutes looked like they were ancient Scots, and they probably sounded like them, too. Besides, wouldn't a backwoods cult this big have been found by the authorities before now?

Of course, time travel was impossible.

But wasn't it also impossible that she'd jumped from a waterfall and ended up in a pond?

There was no chance to think the crazy thought through. The brute moved closer, with a fury in his eyes she didn't like. Hoping to calm him as she did many of her disagreeable patients, she used her best nurse tone and said, "I'm sorry, but you gave me no choice. You refused to stop." She lifted her chin another inch, doing her best to appear strong and bold.

Grasping her by the shoulders, Black Brann lifted her into the air with a huge roar. The men around her joined in, making a ruckus unlike anything she'd ever heard. She was about to kick the big guy in his teeth, but to her surprise, he set her back down in front of him.

Black Brann had scared the shit out of her, but he hadn't harmed a hair on her head. Who was this man?

He moved closer, his eyes boring into hers. "What accent is that ye have? If I'd understood yer strange words, I may have stopped a bit quicker, but I've nae heard that exact talk before."

Something about his green eyes grabbed her, and not in the way she'd expected. They were the strangest shade of green she'd ever seen, like the color of a fresh lime. His admittedly dirty hair was thick and dark brown, and he had a chiseled jaw and a dimple on one cheek. The closer he came, the warmer she became, a strange heat coursing through her as though she were attracted to him.

Dammit, she *was*—his masculinity, his strength, and his brawn overheated her.

No way, Allie. He's a brute.

She was flushed from exertion. That was all it was.

Two men next to her began to ramble in a for-eign tongue, a guttural twist that was unfamiliar to her, as if they'd sooner spit the words out than speak them.

He nodded to them. "'Tis Gaelic they speak, and

I speak Scots, which is a bit newer to all, but I dinnae know what ye speak. 'Tis no' like the English I hate." His gaze traveled down her length, lingering on her clothing. "And what ye wear is a wee bit tight, 'tis nae? Or do ye wish to give yer wares away?"

A little boy yelled, "Brann, she's frightened. Be a wee bit kinder." He pushed ahead of the big brute. He was a cute kid of around eight or ten, freckles across his nose and red hair. "Where are ye from, lass? My name is Lachie and this is my brother, Brann. He's laird of Clan MacKay."

The crowd of men clustered closer to her, the vile smell of unwashed skin and clothing overwhelming her senses enough that her vision blurred. Too close, they were all standing too close. Her claustrophobia kicked in, further blurring her vision.

The big man, Brann, shouted, "Back. All of ye leave now. I'll deal with the lass."

They moved away slowly, apparently too slowly, because the man called Brann pulled a giant sword out from something near his hip. He brandished it at the men who crowded around them, scattering them in various directions. Only the young boy stayed.

The panicky feeling amped up. That sword looked real. She could barely stand, so when he took her hand, she let him.

"Lass, come. Sit for a moment." He led her over to a tree stump and she sat down, only then realizing she'd walked for a good distance without any water.

"Drink?" she asked, hoping he'd understand the simple word.

He grabbed something from his horse, and her thirst was so great that she took a sip without asking what it was, but she gagged and promptly spat it out. "What is that? Have you no water?"

"Ale. 'Tis my best ale ye just spat all over. Dinnae waste good ale. Lachie, get the lass some water." The boy ran off and Brann yelled after him, giving her the perfect opportunity to stare at the laird without being too obvious. If he hadn't been covered in dirt and sweat, he wouldn't be bad looking at all.

Okay, he was hot…even with the dirt and sweat. He didn't smell like the others, so she hoped it was one day's dirt instead of countless days' accumulation.

He spun back around to face her, his expression serious. "Where did ye come from and what do ye want? If ye're selling yer wares, say so now before my brother returns. I'll no' subject him to yer kind."

She gasped at the insinuation and bolted off the log, her arm swinging so fast that she caught half his cheek with a resounding slap, though he saw it coming this time and did his best to stop her.

"Och, 'tis twice now ye've hit me. Stop or I'll return it."

"You called me a whore." Allie had never been so insulted. Her clothes were completely modest, and this stranger, who'd been a part of that strange mob, had seen fit to insult her. "How could you think such a thing? You insulted me, and straight to my face."

He moved his face to about an inch away from hers, doing his best to intimidate her, but she refused to buckle. His words came out in a whisper between clenched teeth. "What do ye wish for me to think when ye come here dressed as ye are, with yer clothes all wet and clinging to ye and the tightest pair of trews I've ever seen."

She gasped, her eyes widening at the realization that he really meant it. He absolutely thought she was a whore.

She had to get the hell out of here, wherever here was.

Allie brushed stray hairs away from her face in frustration, yet she refused to be intimidated by the big brute. "Please just let me use your phone. I need to call my sisters, and then I'll be on my way. I'm lost and I don't know how to get back to them."

"Ye want what? My home?"

"No, your phone. P–H–O–N–E. Phone. Just one call is all I need. Please?"

"I know no' of what ye speak, lass. I have nae phone or whatever 'tis."

She was going to faint for certain.

He wasn't lying.

She could tell by the look on his face that he had no idea what she asked of him. This wasn't a matter of not having a phone or choosing to make war on technology. He literally didn't know what a phone was. She watched as Lachie ran back with a skin of water, taking in the clothing he wore—a plaid garment wrapped in pleats around him, a tunic underneath. Wool socks, boots in this weather. The clothing was weird, no doubt about that, but weird in a special way. Weird like the clothing she'd seen in movies from long ago or the kilts she'd seen in museums. She'd been to a Scottish novelty store full of brightly colored tartans, their carefully stitched pleats arranged just so.

She glanced around the clearing again. The people she'd found weren't the only oddities around here. How had she not noticed before?

No electricity. No poles. No cars, no planes in the sky.

No roads.

No signs or paved sidewalks.

And no females.

She motioned for Lachie to come closer. When he did, she grabbed the end of the fabric he had tossed over his shoulder, tugging it down to look at the stitching. Much as she tried, she couldn't contain her gasp. She moved closer to Brann, reaching for the sleeve of his tunic, then the fabric of his kilt, staring at the hemmed edges up close.

Roughly placed hand stitches bound the ends and held the seams.

Who sewed men's garments by hand?

Thoughts of her favorite Jennae Vale books raced through her mind again. Her voice came out in a croak. "What year is it?"

"What?" Lachie asked.

"What year? You know…fifteen hundred, nineteen hundred, two thousand and eighteen?"

The Scots both grinned and chuckled as if she'd told a grand joke.

"What are ye talking about?" Brann asked.

Lachie laughed. "Two thousand? 'Tis the year of our Lord thirteen ninety-four."

Allie promptly fainted.

CHAPTER THREE

W HEN ALLIE OPENED HER EYES, the first thing she noticed was the strong male body behind her. Her first impression was that she was lying in her bed, spooning with her boyfriend, Chad. She'd had this horrific dream that she'd time-traveled back to medieval Scotland, to a land of fighting, smelly Highlanders. Thank goodness it had only been a dream, even though the big laird had been hot in a brutal kind of way.

There was only one problem. She'd split with her boyfriend two weeks ago, and the body behind her was definitely more muscular than Chad's thin frame.

She sat up, wiping the little bit of drool caught in one corner of her mouth.

"Drooling, lassie?"

She straightened up, just then realizing she sat atop a huge horse, about as far from the ground as if she were riding an elephant. She whipped her head around and wailed as soon as her gaze caught his.

"Nooooooo…" Her hands flew to both sides of her head, as if she could stop the instant ache between her temples. Her head shook side to side as if controlled by someone else.

"Och, if ye dinnae stop, ye'll knock us both off." He grabbed her hips to still her, but she shoved back at him.

The next moment, she was grappling to stay on top of the horse as he cursed her. "Keep still, will ye nae? Ye're upsetting my horse and 'tis a long way down."

The beast shook his head and she grabbed his mane, hoping to stay on. "Okay, I'll keep still." She patted the horse, doing her best to calm him. "What's his name?"

"His name is Star, and he's a warhorse. He doesnae do well with lasses, so stay calm or he'll send us both flying." Brann's hand still held her hip as if to protect her.

"Where are we going?" she whispered, deciding she needed to accept this man's help for the moment. He was a Highlander, and if her favorite novels had served her correctly, he would be honorable, rough, and stubborn, but he would treat her well.

"I'm taking ye to my land. 'Tis nearly dusk and ye can sleep. We'll talk in the morn. Mayhap after a night's rest ye'll remember how ye came to be here."

She glanced over her shoulder, noticed he still carried his sword. About a dozen horses followed his, and the little boy—Lachie he'd been called— waved at her from one of them. The other men in the group were also armed. This was a different crowd from the group she'd seen before. These men looked to be powerful warriors. They sat their horses like beasts, ready to attack anyone who came near them.

She was pleased to notice the vile smells had dissipated. That was of great help to her claustrophobia.

Maybe Brann was right. If she rested, she'd have a better chance of figuring out what had happened to her. She could ask about the area she'd awoken in. Maybe they'd know something.

Until then, there was little point in panicking. Whether this was a delusion—or, God forbid, actual time travel—she may as well enjoy herself as best she could. It would give her the strength to find her sisters, because no matter what had happened, she *would* find them. She wouldn't accept anything less. But if she allowed herself to wonder what had happened to them and where they were, she wouldn't be able to think of anything else.

She leaned back against the Highlander's massive chest and tucked her head under his chin, taking in the beautiful scenery around her. They followed the lane through a dense forest, the only sounds from the scattering of wildlife being interrupted. If it had been daylight, she guessed she'd be able to see the squirrels scampering through the trees while foxes chased rabbits for dinner. She heard the hoot of an owl, which competed only with the most peaceful silence she'd ever heard.

The horses' hooves trampled the path as they moved forward, finally breaking through the trees to a vision unlike anything she'd ever seen before.

"Ye like my castle, lass?"

She turned to nod at Brann, forcing a smile. "It's quite beautiful, especially at night." Perfectly true, but it was also frightening. There were no lights visible. No streetlights, no glow in the windows, no carriage lamps.

Just torches.

Added to the seemingly untouched wilderness they'd traveled through, this lack of lighting seemed to support her insane time travel theory. So did the path they traveled, lined with medieval-style huts.

She'd heard about reenactments put on for tourists or history buffs, but surely they weren't this concerned with authenticity.

"Welcome to Clan MacKay," Brann said. "These are my people. They'll treat ye well as long as ye dinnae kick them in the bollocks or slap them for speaking."

She blushed a deep scarlet, remembering what she'd done to him. "About that. I suppose I should apologize, but the other men would not stop touching me, and I…"

His finger came from behind to settle against her lips, silencing her. "I dinnae fault ye for protecting yerself and yer honor. Ye have my apologies for calling ye what I did. Clearly ye're nae. I wrapped ye in my spare plaid so my clanmates would nae think less of ye for being so bare."

She couldn't help but roll her eyes at his comment, jeans and a peasant top hardly qualified as 'bare,' but if this were truly medieval times, she understood why her clothes looked so odd to him.

Or maybe this was part of some immersive game show, and they gave prizes out to the most convincing reenactors.

If so, all of these people deserved trophies.

As they moved through the huts, people emerged from them and stood on the path, staring at her.

"We know everyone here. They stare at ye because ye are a newcomer."

And stare they did. She noticed the younger girls stared more at Brann than at her. Those who did look at her seemed to be assessing her out of jealousy.

"Are you married?" she whispered, the number of girls gawking at him increasing the farther they moved down the path.

"Nay, and never will be."

That comment took her by surprise, so she peeked back at him, only to be greeted by a stony face. He clearly wasn't ready to explain his answer, so she kept quiet. What did it matter? She was leaving as soon as she could figure out how to get back to her sisters. Even if she had somehow traveled through time, there would be some way to get back. These things always went both ways, right?

A few people shouted at Brann in Gaelic, and from his sharp replies, also in Gaelic, she guessed the questions were about her.

"They're nosy, aren't they?" she tittered, watching the hopeful faces. If she really were in medieval Scotland, she'd say the art of gossip started a very long time ago.

"Nosy? I dinnae know that expression." He gave her a crooked smile, but one that brought the one dimple out, making him even more appealing.

"Wanting to know your business," she explained as she studied the crowd again, not taking her eyes away from the women who glared at her. "And my business, apparently."

"Aye, 'tis natural for them to wonder about their leader. Do ye nae worry about yers?"

She thought about attempting to explain anything about the United States and their president but decided it would be a total waste of her time.

Little boys chased them as they approached the castle, peppering Lachie, who rode directly behind them, with questions. They crossed a small bridge and drew up to the wall that surrounded the castle. The gate was open, but Brann slowed enough to chat with his men, all big, all muscular, all carrying swords, just as many of the men traveling with them did.

She was in the land of Highland giants.

She finally allowed herself to think on her sisters. What had happened to them? Were they back in modern Scotland wondering where she had gone, or had they time traveled to somewhere else in Scotland? What if they'd gone to a different time period? Those thoughts prompted a roiling in her belly she didn't like. Maybe she'd mention the possibility of time travel to her host in the morning, see if he'd heard of it happening to anyone else.

Brann ran his hand down his face. Hellfire, but he was going to have to beat some faces in to get his men to stand down. Several warriors had followed him all the way to the castle gates just to take a good look at his new guest.

Two horses would ride up on either side of him, as close as they dared, before he had to glare at them to get them to hold back. What was happening? One lass had arrived and they'd totally lost their control.

He snorted. They were his warriors, and control was not one of their best features.

Still, he couldn't allow them to continue staring. He let out a shrill whistle. "Get on with yer duties, men."

They shuffled away as innocently as they could. Had she any idea what trouble she was causing? Glancing at her from the side, he had to admit it didn't seem likely. She stared straight ahead, lost in thought and oblivious to all that took place around her.

"Yer name again?"

"Allison Sutton. Allie for short. My sisters call me Allie."

"I've never heard of Clan Sutton. Do yer parents live in a small village on their own? Mayhap ye've come from the Lowlands. Is that yer land, Allison?" He led his horse over to the stables, shooing away all his gawking clanmates.

"From the Lowlands? Sure. That sounds as good as anything, I guess. I have no memory of how I landed where I did. I must have been hit on the head. I jumped into a waterfall and woke up in a strange, warm pool, but I have no idea how I got there. So I walked until I found people."

Brann felt as if he'd been struck by lightning. Could this truly be happening? He could not deny the lass's story fit with the tale his sire had told him years ago. So did her strange attributes—her brash attitude, her peculiar clothes and accent. If there was even a chance it was true, there was only one thing he could do. Help her. He thought on it for a few moments, and finally said, "We'll tell them ye were traveling from the Lowlands when a group of reivers set on ye. All yer companions were killed or ran off, and ye were hit on the head. They left ye to die and we found ye. Or ye found us. Does that suit ye, Allison?"

"Allie. Please call me Allie."

"I've never heard the name before, yet I've heard of many Allisons. 'Tis best for ye to be Allison. Fewer questions will be asked." He dismounted and helped her down, admiring how comely she looked in the green and blue MacKay plaid. Once he set her down, she nearly toppled over, so he set her to rights while Lachie came up behind them.

"Ye've got riders' legs, lass. Have ye nae ridden a horse of late?"

She shook her head.

He turned her around, his hand at her lower back just because he wanted it there, and she didn't fight him fortunately. His second flew out of the keep, heading straight for him across the cobblestone courtyard.

"Brann, how did ye do in the challenge—" He stopped suddenly, as soon as his gaze landed on Allison. "Ye brought a lass home from the corners?"

A strange sense of possessiveness overtook him, and he tugged her back closer to him. She didn't resist.

"We found her no' far from the fields. She and her companions were traveling from the Lowlands to meet their kin when they were set upon by reivers. She has nae memory of what happened. Do ye, lass?"

She shook her head, strangely quiet compared to how she'd been before.

"Find Jinty. Have her make up a chamber for the lass, the one next to mine."

"Next to yers?" He'd never seen his second display such an expression of disbelief. He waited for him to recover.

"Aye, next to mine, Angus. Can ye do that? And this is Allison. She took a blow to the head and 'tis aching her now. Have Jinty give her a concoction to ease her pain."

"Oh no. No concoction," Allison insisted.

"I thought ye said ye have a headache? Jinty will fix ye up right away."

"No. It's better. I just need to rest."

"This is my second in command, Angus. If ye've need of anything, he can assist ye. Jinty is my housekeeper. She also serves as a lady's maid, but since we have verra few ladies in residence at the keep, she does no' do it often. We have two serving maids who also assist in the kitchens. One of them is Jinty's daughter, Elspeth. Be patient with them, if ye would. Angus, find Jinty and stop yer staring."

He led Allison up the steps to the keep, then held the door for her as she stepped inside.

"Down to yer left, ye can warm up near the hearth. Sit there and I'll bring ye some ale."

"No, thank you. No ale. Do you have any wine?"

"Nay." he said, unable to hide his shock. Wealthy women knew of wine, but he wouldn't have guessed her to be wealthy. "Mead?"

"Could I have a cup of both ale and mead to see which one I like better?" She folded her hands in front of her, a timid position compared to how she'd acted before. His bollocks still ached from the kick she'd given him.

"Ye dinnae know?"

"No. We drank wine, water, and…milk at home."

"We have milk to break our fast with," he said slowly. "Pour it in our porridge sometimes. I'll find ye something. I'll be right back."

He left his great hall out the back door and headed to the kitchens. What the hell kind of clan drank wine, water, and milk? The strangeness of her request, and all the words she spoke, only made him more suspicious that she was the one.

He found Angus just inside the kitchens, talking with Cook and Jinty. Jinty's daughter and the other serving lass listened, but they scuttled away upon seeing him. The remaining three stopped talking as soon as he entered. He already knew exactly what they wanted to know.

"I know no' what to tell ye all. She wandered onto the corner fields, confused and scared. Was I to leave her there for the entertainment of those men full of ale? Had I turned my back on her for a moment, they'd have been fondling her with plans of mounting her soon. I wouldnae allow that. Lachie took a shine to her, so I brought her here. She doesnae remember what happened. I thought to give her a good night's rest, and we'll find out more on the morrow. Do ye have a problem with my decision? Any of ye?"

All three shook their heads in unison before Cook spun around to finish her work. "Here's a meat pie for the lass. I have a berry tart or two left. Lassies like sweet things." She made a tray and handed it to Jinty.

"I need two goblets, one with a touch of mead and the other with a touch of ale."

Cook quirked her brow at him but said nothing.

"The lass cannae remember which she likes. Is that a bother?"

"Nay, of course no', my lord." Cook hurried to do as she was bid, putting three goblets on the tray. "One for ye, my lord. Ye look like ye need one."

"Jinty, will ye see that the chamber is made up for her?"

"Aye, my lord." He explained how he wanted it prepared, and Jinty hurried out to see to her duties.

No truer statement had ever been made. What was he to do with the lass on the morrow?

And how the hell was he to protect her from a clan full of men with barely enough women around and loins ready to burst?

He was in for a long night.

CHAPTER FOUR

A LLIE SMILED AND STOOD UP from the
trestle table. She'd only managed a couple of
bites of the meat pie, the stringy meat inside doing
a number on her belly, but the fruit tart had been
quite tasty. It would do her for the night. "Thank
you for your hospitality. I think I'll rest now, if you
don't mind. Where shall I sleep?"

Brann said, "Jinty will be right along to show ye
to yer chamber. She's making the bed up for ye."

"I can help. Where's the room?" She was about
to head up the staircase at the end of the large hall
when she caught sight of a tiny gray puppy with
curly fur stumbling near the back doorway. Lachie
sat on the floor near it, next to a large crate. The
sound of soft cries told her it was full of more pup-
pies. "Oh, how sweet!"

She'd always loved dogs, but her sisters were both
cat lovers. Since their two votes had counted more
than her one, her parents had gotten them a cat
when they were young. Since she'd wanted a dog
and hadn't gotten her way, she'd been given the

chore of naming the cat.

She'd named it Kitty just to annoy them. Oh, how her sisters had teased her.

As she stooped to pick up the little one, Lachie jumped up from the crate he sat next to in the corner. "Dinnae touch her. Leave her be. Her mother dinnae want her."

Allie couldn't heed that, so she scooped the pup up and held her against her chest. "Your mama does not want you? But you're so cute."

Brann appeared next to her, explaining, "She's the runt. Her mother will take her outside, where she'll die quickly."

"Die quickly? Have you no heart?" Allie's gaze moved from one expectant face to the other. Both of them had clearly planned to leave the puppy to die. "Really? You'd just let her die?"

Brann quirked his brow at her. "'Tis the way of animals. They leave the runt to die. Every litter."

"I don't care if it's the way," she snapped. "I'll keep her. Just give me some milk, and I'll feed her myself." Turning to Lachie, certain she'd find an ally in him, she said, "You agree with him?"

He slowly nodded, his eyes wide. "Brann says 'tis the way."

Incredulous, she stared at him in shock, then shifted her gaze back to his brother, certain he was to blame.

"But that's so archaic…" Her words fell off as she stared back and forth between the two of them. She brushed a strand of hair back from her face with exasperation, the only way she could properly display her mood without upsetting anyone.

Brann reached for the pup, but Allie wouldn't

have it. "Don't touch her. She's mine."

"Ye are only prolonging the inevitable." He'd moved close enough to unnerve her a bit, just because…

Well, dammit. No use lying to herself. The Highlander had her hormones raging.

When was the last time she'd felt this drawn to a man? She'd liked her last boyfriend in the beginning, but there hadn't been any passion between them. Nothing like this, anyway. This man made her think of those steamy romance books she loved…and want to act them out.

"I'm a nurse. I'll take care of her." She dared them to challenge her. When her nursing persona took over, she didn't budge.

Lachie's eyes widened and he turned to Brann, who was doing his best to hide a smile.

"Ye mean ye're nursing, lass?" His smirk couldn't be contained as his gaze dropped to her breasts.

This language barrier was getting annoying. "I'm not nursing, and I've never been pregnant. I don't have any kids either."

Lachie gave her the most serious expression she'd ever seen before. "What do goats have to do with the puppy?"

She closed her eyes in frustration before an idea struck. "I need goat's milk for the pup. I'll feed her. That's all I'll need. Then I'll go to my room."

"Yer chamber?" He tipped his head toward her in confusion.

"Yes, my chamber." Dammit.

"May I find her some goat's milk, Brann? I hate it when the runts die." The expression of love and respect in the boy's eyes caught her. The man was good with his brother, so she'd have to excuse his treatment of the pup.

Brann gave him a slight nod and waved him off toward the kitchens—or so she guessed. If she recalled her history lessons at all, there would be a large, hot, stifling set of kitchens attached to the back of the keep. They had to have multiple hearths in order to prepare food for so many.

She cuddled the pup under her chin. "I'll take care of her. As soon as I get the milk, I'll go to my chamber and I'll not bother you again. Which one is it?"

"The top of the stairs, second door on the right. The chamber next to mine."

He'd said as much before, but it hadn't stood out to her. Now she couldn't help but wonder what it meant.

Suddenly, she felt exhausted and all thoughts of sex with the warrior in front of her vanished. Tired of trying to fight her way out of an impossible situation, and of verbally sparring with this Highland warrior in front of her, she just wanted to go to sleep and find her sisters. In fact, she couldn't fight the tears welling in her eyes.

Brann noticed.

She closed her eyes and tucked the pup closer, wishing and praying her situation would revert to normal.

But it didn't.

"Lass, I did no' mean any impropriety." His thumb reached up to brush a tear away from her cheek. "I want only to help ye, whatever be yer situation."

She froze at his touch, but then decided to allow

it. Despite the fact that she'd literally greeted him with a blow to the balls, he'd assisted her from the beginning. True, he teased her at times, but somehow she knew he would always help her—all she had to do was ask.

If only she knew how to explain the truth to him. She nodded and turned away as soon as Lachie arrived with a bowl of goat's milk. The housekeeper came down the stairs, slow enough to indicate some possible arthritis, but she guessed her to be a hard worker nonetheless.

"This is Jinty," the boy said. "She'll lead ye to yer chamber abovestairs."

"Yes, I met her before we ate. Thank you for all your help, both of you." She glanced back at Brann to include him in the remark. "I'll try to explain everything after I've rested some."

She followed Jinty up the staircase and down the candlelit passageway to her room. When she stepped inside, she marveled at how much the stone-walled room looked like something out of a movie set. A real fire crackled in the hearth, a chest stood at the foot of the simple bed, and a colorful tapestry hung on the wall above the furniture. She was surprised at the sweet aroma.

"What is that scent?" she asked.

Jinty said, "I gave ye the heather-stuffed mattress, my lady. 'Tis acceptable to ye?"

"Jinty, I'm not a …you don't have to call me…" What the hell did she know about this time period? Maybe she *did* need to call her that.

The maid bustled around the room. "My lord brought a chair in for ye to sit near the fire to stay warm. There are plenty of plaids and a few furs to keep ye warm during the night. There's an ewer of water on the table, and yer pot is—" she glanced one direction and then the other before she finished, "—behind the wee screen there."

Allie couldn't help but sigh over another convenience she'd have to do without. "That's right, you don't have any bathrooms, do you? No showers?" She found the chamber pot as promised. The pup whined and squirmed a bit in her arms. "Wait. What do you use if there's no toilet paper?"

Jinty plucked at the hairs escaping her plait, her slight smile dimming with confusion. She wore a plain gray gown, well-worn over her ample hips, and looked to be about forty years old. "I'm sorry, my lady. What is it ye want? I dinnae understand yer words."

She pointed to the chamber pot, hoping the older woman would understand.

What was she to wipe with?

"Och, here. Follow me. I'll show ye where the garderobe is."

"Garderobe?" She was in trouble, but then she reminded herself that as a nurse, she could handle anything. She'd dealt with everything as a floor nurse in the hospital. Puke, pee…you name it. She took a deep breath, giving the pup a little comforting squeeze, and followed Jinty down to the end of the passageway. The maid stopped and pointed to an alcove with a hole in a seat.

"That's it? No door?"

"Och," Jinty said, tugging on the curtain and pulling it shut to demonstrate how she could shield herself. "The lads never use it, but ye may. Here are some linen squares for yer tender sensibilities." She showed her the spot where they kept the linens and another spot where she could toss the used ones.

Oh, but she desperately needed to go back to her time. Her pulse sped up, but she forced herself to ignore it. In fact, she didn't have to think like a nurse here. They didn't even know what a nurse was, they only had healers. The word nurse conjured up breastfeeding mothers for them.

"Thank you, Jinty. I'll take the puppy back to my chamber now. We're a bit tired."

"I brought a small crate for the pup, threw in some old blankets for her. She'll pee all over the bed if ye dinnae put her inside."

Allie nodded and smiled. "I expect you are correct. Thank you. That was thoughtful of you."

"Och, I almost forgot. My daughter Elspeth is nearly yer size. I left a night rail and a couple of gowns in the chest for ye to wear. It seems ye dinnae come with much. If ye've need of anything else, please let me or my daughter know."

She watched, feeling more than a little out of sorts, as Jinty hurried down the passageway and headed down the stairs.

As soon as she was back in the room, with the door firmly shut behind her, Allie held the pup out as if it were human. "I think I'll call you Smoky," she said. "Hannah wanted to call our kitten Smoky, but I wouldn't let her. For her sake, I hope she's still in the twenty-first century. She'll be very upset if she has to use a garderobe." She cuddled the pup up close to her chest. "Oh, Smoky, what will I do? I hope Hannah and Caroline are back in Scotland, going back to our inn."

She sat down in the chair with a huff. She located the bowl of goat's milk, found a linen square, and twisted the corner of it until it looked like it would fit into the puppy's mouth. She dipped it into the milk and then held it in the pup's mouth. "Come on, wee Smoky. I know my sister Hannah doesn't like milk, but you must." Just as she'd hoped, the pup tasted a couple of drops of milk, which prompted her to start suckling on the linen as though it were her mother's teat.

It took a while, but little Smoky took quite a bit of the milk. She blinked sleepily up at Allie, as if declaring she was now ready for bed, and Allie set her down on one of the blankets in the crate. The little puppy curled up and promptly fell asleep.

A quick search of the chest yielded a nightgown. It appeared to be clean, made of linen, so she removed her clothes and Brann's plaid to change.

The lump in one of the pockets of her jeans surprised her—she'd totally forgotten about her homemade survival pack. Brimming with excitement, she pulled out the zipped plastic bag she'd used to protect her things before the jump.

She set her jeans near the fire to dry, though they'd mostly dried already. Checking the other pockets of her clothes, she was pleased to find a few other items. She lined them all up on her table and smiled at her small treasures, all invaluable to an RN: hand sanitizer; a small container of naproxen pills for headaches, pain or fever; a miniscule container of amoxicillin pills; a few Band-Aids; and three emergency condoms, one for her and each of her sisters. Last but not least was a little vial of penicillin her nurse practitioner friend had insisted she take on the trip. She'd also given her two syringes, but those had remained in her luggage because they'd broken and were now useless.

As a nurse, she knew very well how fast bacterial infections could kill, and her friend had told her how hard it would be to get a doctor to prescribe anything for them in a foreign country.

She couldn't help but chuckle. How her sisters had teased her for carrying her survival pack everywhere, especially since she'd left her phone and wallet locked up in the car. But she'd just waggled her finger at the two of them and said, "Someday…someday you'll see."

If only her sisters were standing next to her so she could have the final say.

What was the fun in being right if she couldn't brag about it to the two people she loved most of all?

She located a small sack in the chest and hid her belongings inside. Whatever she did, she'd have to make sure her things were never discovered by anyone in this century.

Dammit, she was thinking as if this were truly the fourteenth century, but it couldn't be, could it?

It just couldn't.

Once she'd hidden her goodies, she undressed and put on the fine linen gown, quite different than the sweatpants and T-shirt she normally wore to bed, but at least it was clean.

What was she supposed to do tomorrow with no clean undergarments?

She climbed onto the surprisingly soft mattress and pulled Smoky's crate over next to her. After piling the stack of furs on top of her, she fell asleep in seconds, completely exhausted.

And praying that she would wake up and discover this was all somehow a dream.

CHAPTER FIVE

B RANN WOKE UP IN THE middle of the night to an odd sound. Someone was crying not far away. He shook his head to clear the fog from his brain and listened intently.

A lass sobbed, her breath hitching every moment or so. Since there were so few lasses in the keep, and they spent much of their time near the kitchens, it had to be Allison. Hellfire, but he hated it when women cried. He sat up, listening to the sound as it began to drift away.

She was headed down the stairs.

He grabbed his plaid and arranged the pleats over his bare body. Though his preference would have been to go with nothing on, he didn't wish to startle her.

As soon as he was covered, he made haste down the stairs, climbing over some of his warriors who'd chosen to sleep on the floor in the great hall, the snores and occasional snorts not disturbing him in the least. What had Allison thought when she'd entered the hall? By her own account, she did not hail from a normal clan.

There was no sign of her in the cavernous space, so he opened the door to the outside. A cool gust of wind greeted him, but he didn't slow his walk, moving toward the courtyard until he froze at the vision before him.

She stood in a night rail directly in front of the largest torches they had, her body silhouetted so perfectly from the side that the sight shot straight to his loins. Long legs, pert breasts, and long blonde hair that would haunt him later in his sleep.

He reminded himself that she was a woman the same as any other, one who would dishonor him without a care. He'd never marry after what Shona had done to him. With that thought in mind, his erection disappeared and he moved forward to see what she was about.

He followed her over to the grass on the side of the cobblestones, only then seeing the puppy. Ah, he realized, she'd come outside to allow the wee runt to do her sniffing. She'd been so stubborn about the small animal. If it hadn't been for the hopeful look in Lachie's eyes, perhaps he would have been more insistent.

He'd known right away it would be a battle, and it just wasn't worth it. The lass needed sleep so she could remember what had happened to her.

The only problem was Allison sniffed quite a bit more than the pup. She settled on a rock nearby while the puppy scampered around, looking for just the right spot to take care of her needs.

He knew the moment she saw him because she started and swiped the tears from her face in a hurry. "Is anything wrong, lass, or did ye just come out for the puppy to relieve herself?"

"I'm fine. Sorry to have bothered you."

"Nae bother. I was awake already," he fibbed, not wishing to make her feel any worse than she already did. He pointed to a bench under an oak tree not far away and held his hand out to her. "Come, we can sit together over here. No one will hear us, and I'd like to ask ye a few questions."

She sniffled, but she took his hand and followed him to the bench.

"I couldnae help but overhear yer sobs from the chamber next to mine. What has saddened ye so?"

She took a deep breath as she sat down, pulling her hand free. "I seriously thought I was living a dream, but I woke up and found nothing had changed. Here I am in a strange land with no one to trust, and I have no idea what to do. I don't know what happened to my sisters, nor do I have any idea how to find out. I've never felt so helpless in all my life."

"But I told ye I'd help ye on the morrow. Did ye no' believe me?" He reached for her hand, intertwining their fingers, and used the thumb of his other hand to trace tiny circles on her soft skin. He found he liked touching her, but he told himself he did it simply to comfort her, no other reason.

"I do believe you." She stared at their linked hands, then lifted her gaze to his. "But I don't know if you can help me. The world I came from is so different."

"Of course I can help. Why would ye think that I cannae?"

She paused before she answered. "Because you'll never believe what I have to say. No one would believe me. I don't believe the story myself. It's impossible." She stared off into the distance.

"May I tell ye a story before ye say that?" He'd never revealed this to anyone, but he felt more and more confident there was a connection between his sire's account and what had happened to Allison. Perhaps the time had finally come to speak of it.

"I have nowhere else to go but here," she said. The puppy scampered closer but continued to play in the grass, rolling on her back with a glee that brought a smile to Allison's face, a smile that made her quite beautiful.

"My sire passed on two years ago, four years after my mother passed. He'd taken a bad wound, and he feared he'd not survive, so he asked to speak to me alone. What he told me, I've never shared with anyone."

"Really? Why not?"

"Because his words were such that I dinnae believe him. I never have believed what he shared. I thought it a foolish suggestion from a dying man's mind, but now I wonder if I was wrong."

"Go on, please." He could see he had her complete attention.

He took a deep breath and plunged ahead, hoping he wasn't making a big mistake. The last thing he needed was for the lass to think him daft. "He told me to guard the faerie pool on our land. 'Tis a beautifully warm pool that sits hidden amongst rocks no' far from where I met ye at the corner fields. Papa said I should always protect it."

He could feel her hand tremble beneath his. Her reaction prompted him to continue. "He fell in and out of consciousness for two days, and on one occasion, he looked at me and said, 'Promise me, Breannainn. Promise me ye will always protect the faerie pool. 'Tis where I found yer mother.'

"I said, 'Papa, we know Mama loved to swim in the pool. I'll protect it for her memory.'"

He swallowed, unable to believe he was about to admit this to her. "Then he said, 'Nay, son. Mama is a faerie. She came from another land through that portal, a land in the future. I had to convince her to stay with me and not go back. She stayed because she carried ye, and ye belong in this time. I tell ye so if ye ever see another near that pool, an unusual person, know it may not be what it seems.' He closed his eyes again. I tried to get him to tell me more because it seemed nonsense, but he wouldn't stir. A quarter of an hour later, he awakened and said, 'Another faerie will come through the portal. Mama told me 'twould be yer job to protect her when she comes. I never wished to tell ye, but now, since my time is near, I must. I never believed her, but what if she was telling the truth?'"

Her hands shook so violently he tightened his grip on them, trying to calm her.

"No, no, no…" Her gaze darted from him to the pup to the moon up above. "It cannot be true."

He did what he thought was best to keep her calm. "Where are ye from, lass? I promise to believe ye and no' to tell another."

Tears brimmed her eyes and she grabbed him with a death grip. "No…"

"At the time, I thought my sire was daft from the fever, but now I wonder…" Allison had a strange expression on her face, of disbelief or even horror.

He had to make her see that it could not be that bad. "Allison?"

She stared at him in disbelief, still shaking her head.

"Where are ye from? England? The East? Are ye Welsh? Norse?"

"No," she said, "and as you've guessed, I'm not from the Lowlands either. I…if I tell you the truth, I'm afraid you'll think I'm mad."

He moved closer and wrapped his arm around her shoulder, hoping to ease her trembling. "I'll no' think ye are daft. I promise to keep yer secret, but I cannae help ye if I dinnae know all."

She leaned in, resting her head on his shoulder, and whispered close to his ear. "I jumped into a waterfall in Scotland in the twenty-first century, and I landed in the faerie pool here. I have two sisters. We lost our parents a year ago, so we decided to take a trip to Scotland to honor them. My little sister begged us to jump into this waterfall with her, Leannan Falls. Hannah, she's my older sister, and I didn't want to, but Caroline begged and begged until we agreed. We wanted to land at the base at the same time, so I held her hand and she held Hannah's, but when I came up for air, they were gone."

He didn't say anything. He *couldn't* say anything. If his sire hadn't told him the story of the pond, he never would have believed her, but it could hardly be a coincidence that the very thing his sire had warned him of had happened. "The twenty-first century would be the year two thousand and something," he mumbled, the words rolling over his tongue and churning in his mind.

She continued, her head still on his shoulder. "I looked around the pool and everything was different than when we'd jumped. Before, there was only a small rock or two at the base of a tall waterfall, but there are boulders all the way around your pool and there's no waterfall above it. I didn't know what else to do but to climb out and find someone to help me. So I started walking and your field was the only place I heard noises."

"So ye are a Scots lass from another time. 'Tis nae so bad."

"But I'm not a Scots. We were visiting Scotland. That's where the waterfall was, but that's not where I'm from."

"So where?"

She chewed on her lip before she answered. "The United States. There is no such place in your time period. It didn't develop until way beyond the 1600s."

Neither spoke for a moment. His hand rubbed circles over the skin of her shoulder. What could he say?

The puppy found Allison and tried to climb up her leg. She reached down and picked her up, settling the dog on her lap where she curled up and closed her eyes. "I named her Smoky because my sister wanted to name our cat Smoky. I love my sisters with all my heart and they're both gone." She ran her hand across Smoky's soft fur, lulling her to sleep. "Do you think if I went back to the pool, I could return to my time? I mean, if I were to jump in the water, could whatever happened reverse itself and send me back?"

He'd only heard mention of its powers from his

sire on his deathbed, and he'd thought him daft. "Lass, I cannae answer yer question, but I promise to take ye back so ye can try."

"Will you take me back tomorrow?" She sat up and stared at him, biting her bottom lip.

Truth be told, he'd promise her anything if she kept looking at him like that. "Aye, if I have nae other duties, I'll take ye midday on the morrow."

He would take her because he knew it would be the best for both of them.

But something deep inside told him not to.

CHAPTER SIX

WHEN SHE HEADED DOWN TO eat breakfast, Smoky firmly clasped in her arms, Allie
did her best to contain her excitement. She could
be going back today, through the portal Brann had
told her about.

"Smoky, you'll be big and strong without me. I'll
make Lachie promise to take care of you."

The gray puppy looked up at her and made a
loud mewling sound as she whipped her tail about.

"That was a kitty noise. You are a dog, my dear,
and dogs bark. I know you're little, but we must
work on your bark. I'll go into the kitchens and
find you some milk."

She made her way through the hall, smiling
at all the warriors, who smiled at her in return,
and greeting the serving maids. When she walked
through the back door, she nearly fell off the stoop.
"What the hell?"

Smoky gave a little whelp to remind Allie how
hungry she was. Confused, her gaze searched the
area, settling on a building with smoke streaming

FALLING FOR THE CHIEFTAIN   53

from its chimney.

"I thought the kitchens were through this door," she muttered to the dog.

A door opened in the little building, and Lachie came flying through it with a bowl of some goop. "Good morn to ye, Allison. Are ye headed to the kitchens?"

"Yes, but I thought it was through this door," she said, indicating the threshold behind her. "I guess I need to go back."

Lachie laughed. "Nay, the kitchens are in that building." He pointed to the building with the chimney.

"It's not attached?"

"Nay, 'tis too hot. It could burn the keep down. Follow me. I'll introduce ye to Cook."

She glanced over her shoulder at the building behind her. "Burn it down? But it's made of stone." Her gaze took in the dull gray structure, following it up to maybe the height of three stories, then traveled to the tower in the corner. A thick wall of stones, nearly ten feet tall or more, surrounded the outside of the castle.

"Ye like our curtain wall? Did ye no' have one at home?"

"No—nay," she mumbled, following the wall with her eyes until she was once again looking at the area behind the kitchens. She could swear she'd been on cobblestones in the front courtyard, but the back area seemed comprised of paths between bushes and unkempt plots of grass. Her gaze shifted from the imposing structure back to Lachie's face. "There's a door right over there," she said, pointing to the middle of the curtain wall across the back.

"Aye, 'tis how we escape if we're attacked at the front." Lachie spoke to her as though her wits were addled.

She brought her attention back to the boy in front of her.

"Can you help me find more milk for my puppy?"

"Aye, the goat's milk jug was just filled. Have ye named her yet?" His hand rubbed the dog's head as she tried to sniff his bowl.

"I named her Smoky."

"Then Smoky, I'll get ye a small bowl."

"And another linen square to feed her, if you don't mind." Allie hurried after Lachie, the squirming pup held tight against her, but she almost took a step back when she followed him into the kitchens. "Yikes!"

"Ye see why 'tis separate?" He grinned and took off toward the center of the building. "Cook, our guest needs some porridge and some goat's milk."

A woman's voice said, "Take whate'er ye need, laddie. I'm busy working on the midday meal."

Three other women worked inside—one kneading dough, another washing dishes, and a third chopping vegetables. She would have introduced herself, but with any luck she would be returning home today, so it seemed pointless.

Lachie found a tray and grabbed everything they needed before leading the way back into the great hall. They sat together at a trestle table, and Allie settled Smoky on her lap, twirling the linen square into a model of a teat. "You'll take care of Smoky if anything happens to me, Lachie?"

"Why would anything happen to ye? Ye can take

care of her. She likes ye better."

Rather than argue, she continued to feed the puppy, who drank everything in the bowl. If she did disappear, he would hopefully remember their conversation.

"What plans do you have today, Lachie?"

"I'll go help Brann in the lists."

"The lists?"

"Where our warriors practice their sword skills. Brann gave me a new sword to practice with. Would ye like to join me?"

"Nay, Brann said he would…" She paused, contemplating how she could best explain her goal for the day. "He said he'd show me the area."

"May I come, too?"

"You'll have to ask Brann. I'm not sure." She didn't feel she could speak for him. Brann was a bit different from any of the men she'd known, though being from medieval times would tend to make one stand out.

She ate her porridge, surprised to find it palatable once Lachie gave her a bit of his secret ingredient—honey. The boy hurried away with a quick goodbye, and she was left to herself to consider her situation.

Other than her sisters, who would miss her back home?

No one.

She'd taken time off from her job as a nurse at the hospital, so they wouldn't figure out something had happened to her for days. Chad, the jerk, certainly wouldn't care. She'd broken up with him two weeks before this trip because she'd discovered he was also seeing another woman. In fact, she'd caught him with his pants down, in every way possible.

Chad was another nurse, and she'd found him on top of one of the other nurses in a patient room at work. The only thing she'd said, with the intent of ruining his orgasm, was "Bye, Chad."

Caroline had said it was no great loss, though that was no great surprise. Her sisters never seemed to like her boyfriends.

Truth was, none of the men she'd dated had ever felt like the one. She had an uncanny ability to choose the wrong person. There had only been four boyfriends, but three of the four had cheated on her, and without any apparent guilt.

So her parents were dead, she had no boyfriend, her sisters were who knows where, and her friends were all wrapped up in their own business. No one would wonder where she was except Caroline and Hannah.

A pretty young woman of about sixteen or seventeen came along and introduced herself. "Greetings to ye, my lady. My name is Elspeth. Jinty is my mother. She said ye had a bad experience and lost yer kin. If ye need anything at all, I'd be more than pleased to help ye."

"Thank you, Elspeth."

"Ye talk strangely," the girl said with a slight blush.

"I came from a different place, closer to London, so I have a different accent." How else could she hope to explain it?

"Yer pardon, my lady. I must assist my mother." Then Elspeth leaned down to whisper to her. "I think Brann likes ye. All the lasses here are jealous."

Giggling, she scooped up Allie's dishes.

Allie barely had the chance to thank the young girl before she disappeared from the hall. If she had the chance, she'd have to ask Elspeth a few more questions about Brann.

That is, if she stayed. First, she needed to decide what she was doing. The way Smoky wiggled on her lap, she decided it was probably best to take her outside again. Besides, it would give her an excuse to look for Brann.

She made her way out the door, surprised to see everyone running around in a tizzy, some heading toward the gates and others hurrying in the opposite direction. Though she had no idea what you'd call it in medieval times, "tizzy" seemed like the best word to explain what she was seeing. She found a grassy patch near the curtain wall, away from the others, and set Smoky down in the grass.

She finally had the nerve to stop a rotund woman who was panting pretty heavily. "Is something wrong?" Her nurse's training took over as she counted the woman's respiratory rate, which was just a bit high.

"My lord Taran is here. Oh my. Our chief will no' be happy. I'm off to hide in the garden near the wall."

If she'd wanted to keep the woman next to her, she was quite sure it would have required a fist to the gut to stop her forward progress. What was this about? Who was Taran?

In less than two minutes, two other women followed the first one, so intent on their destination they ignored Allie.

Surprised to hear shouting and cursing near the

gates, she scooped up Smoky and decided to see what all the fuss was about.

Lachie came barreling past her, but he grabbed her hand. "Come up here with me. We're nae big enough to see."

She followed him up to the top of the curtain wall, ascending a narrow staircase built into the stone, so she could peek over the edge.

Brann's loud voice carried to her. "Get the hell out of here, Taran. I've told ye many times ye're not welcome here."

Her position on the wall gave her a perfect view of Brann as he bellowed at a horseman who'd approached the opposite side of the moat with ten guards.

Lachie said, "My brother, Taran. He stole Brann's betrothed, Shona, and Brann will never forgive him."

"I came to mend our differences, Brann. Allow me to talk with ye? May I please sit in our sire's solar, break bread with ye in our parents' hall?"

"Is it just the three of you?" Allie asked.

"Aye. We used to have fun together, but ever since Shona came between them, it has been a nightmare." Lachie's eyes misted. "I care for both of my brothers."

"Brann doesn't expect you to hate Taran, does he? It's his own battle, not yours. And just so you know, if my sister did that to me, I'd be pretty upset, too. I'd get over it, but it would take me a while." She reached over and patted Lachie's shoulder. He was too young to understand romantic jealousy.

Lachie swiped at his tears, stopping them. "Nay, Brann says I dinnae have tae hate Taran. I just wish they'd talk again. Why cannae Taran come here to visit and leave Shona at his castle?"

"Where do they live?"

"Brann gave him the small castle that borders our land. He said 'twas better to have it occupied so nae one attacks it, and he wanted Taran away from here."

Brann stared at his brother for the longest time, silence settling over the gathering. Finally, he said, "Go home, Taran. I dinnae want ye on my land."

"Our sire's land, ye mean, brother." Taran was not going to back down.

"Aye, 'twas our sire's, but now 'tis my own. Go home to yer dear wife, Taran. I'll take care of protecting the Highlands."

"As ye wish for now, Brann, but I'll no' accept it forever. Ye know ye dinnae love Shona. Until ye wish to talk to me as yer brother, I request a visit from Lachie. Lachie?" He tipped his head toward the curtain wall. "I know ye're there. Will ye come for a visit?"

"Aye." Lachie bolted from his spot, then turned back to her. "Apologies, Allison. I must hurry."

"Go," Allie said. "Enjoy your visit." How she hoped Brann would allow it. She peeked back over the wall just as Lachie launched himself through the gates.

"Brann, may I go? I'd like a visit with Taran."

She could almost see the disappointment in Brann's posture, but he surprised her by nodding. "Go, Lachie. Get yer things." Then he shouted at Taran, "I want him back within a sennight."

Taran nodded. "Agreed. I will return him to ye."

Brann turned around and strode back through

his gates, waving to his men to stay until Taran left.

Allie hugged Smoky close and hurried down the staircase, managing to get down quickly enough to follow Brann into the courtyard.

She caught up with him and said, "Brann, you did the right thing."

He spun on his heel and glared at her. His hands went to his hips, his feet braced in a warrior stance. Who was he truly fighting? His brother or himself?

"Did I?" he snarled. "And what if Lachie doesn't return? What if he chooses to leave me and stay with them?" He looked around and then tugged her by the arm over to an oak tree by the curtain wall. As soon as they got there, she set Smoky down on the ground.

"I only allowed you to pull on me because you're upset, but don't think of hurting me, because I won't allow it," she admonished him, hoping he believed her. Just because she was in medieval Scotland did not mean she'd accept being treated like a medieval woman.

The look he gave her was that of a man in emotional torment. "I fear I'll lose both of my brothers."

She shook her head. "Letting him visit with your other brother doesn't mean you'll lose him. He'll appreciate you for allowing him to make up his own mind." Looking him in the eye, she said, "This is on your shoulders. Taran wants to get past your problem."

"My problem? Ye mean his problem, do ye no'?" His jaw clenched as he leaned forward to speak with her. "Tell me the truth. Ye have two sisters. How would ye feel if one stole yer betrothed?"

Dammit. He'd asked her the one question she

didn't wish to answer. She hedged, tipping her head first one way and the other, hoping the small delay would help her come up with the best reply.

"I wouldn't be happy," she finally said.

"Ye wouldnae be happy. 'Tis all ye've got to say abou' it? And wha' would ye say to yer sister?"

She did her best to distract him. "That would depend on which sister did it."

"Why?"

"Because…well…one is older, one is younger…"

"The eldest one. If she stole yer betrothed, they fell in love, and he married her instead, how would ye feel?"

She sighed as dramatically as she could, rolling her eyes. "Shitty."

"Shitty? What does tha' mean? Like a piece of shite?"

"Yes. We call it shit, no' shite."

"Ye curse worse than a reiver," he chuckled, waggling his brow at her.

"You asked me how I'd feel, and I told you."

"Now be honest," he said, his expression serious again. "Would ye nae be full of pish about it?" His face moved to within an inch of her nose.

She shrugged her shoulders. "Fine! I'd be pissed. You're damn right I'd be pissed. And I'd scream at her and…and…"

"And?"

"And I'd probably like to knock her off her feet. There, are you happy?"

He grinned and leaned back. "Aye. 'Tis about time someone was honest with me. Now ye know how I feel. 'Tis a matter of pride."

"But…"

"But what?"

"But I wouldn't stay mad forever. I love my sister too much. Which reminds me. Are you still going to take me to the faerie pool?" She clenched her hands together in front of her to keep herself from begging. "Please?"

So maybe she was willing to beg a bit.

"I'll take ye. Be here in about an hour. I need some time to myself." He spun on his heel and left.

She bent over and picked up the puppy. "Come, sweet one. I'll have to find someone to watch you while I'm gone, especially if I don't return. Lachie will take care of you, but you'll need someone to keep an eye on you until he gets back."

She touched her nose to Smoky's tiny one. "I'll miss you if I go back home." Tears misted her eyes and she chastised herself. "I'm such a sap. You'll be fine without me. I'll make Brann promise not to toss you aside."

Heading back to the great hall, she fell a bit wistful. True, she wished to go back home, especially to see her sisters, but she'd found acceptance here, at least from Brann and Lachie. She had to face the possibility that she may not be able to go back. Brann's mother had never returned to her home, wherever and whenever that was, though she may have chosen not to try. In any case, Allie knew she'd definitely be useful here with her knowledge of nursing. Then she thought of all the things she'd be giving up: hot showers, toilets that flush, cars instead of horses, leggings, ice cream. She'd only been here one night, and this was probably the longest she'd gone without ice cream.

She'd probably be thin if she lived here forever

FALLING FOR THE CHIEFTAIN   63

just because the food was so horrid.

Nope. She was going back. Her mind made up, she headed toward the kitchens with the pup. "You're probably hungry again, little one. Jinty will feed you something nice in the kitchens. She'll take good care of you. It's probably best if you don't get too attached to me."

The pup looked up at her and whined.

"You did that on purpose, Smoky Deerhound. Just like my big sister would—anything to make me feel guilty. Well, I don't. There are patients who need me back home."

The pup gave her the saddest eyes she'd ever seen, and all she could do was scowl in return. "Never mind, you. You belong in this time period. I don't."

A few hours from now, she could be back home.

CHAPTER SEVEN

B RANN SADDLED HIS HORSE HIMSELF just
because he was so fond of the beast. A warrior needed to have a special relationship with his
horse.

He'd chosen ten guards to patrol the periphery
of his land. A laird never traveled alone, but he
didn't plan on leaving MacKay land, so there was
no real threat to his safety if there were no reivers
on his land.

There rarely were since he took swift action
against them.

Allison hurried toward him in a gown he hadn't
seen her in before, one that clung to her curves
in the breeze, and quite nicely if he had to admit.
Jinty had done well.

"Are ye no' taking yer strange clothing back with
ye?"

She held out a rolled bundle of plaid. "I put them
inside this. I'll change when we get there. I didn't
wish to offend any of your clanmates."

He snorted.

"What the hell does that mean?" Her hands plopped on her hips.

"It means I dinnae think ye cared what others think."

"Of course I don't. I hardly know anyone here." Her lips protruded in a pouty look. Funny how he already knew what that meant—she wasn't happy with what he'd said, but she wasn't going to argue the point.

He smirked, still fixing everything on his horse just the way he liked it. "But it matters at home? 'Tis the way of it?"

She thought of his question for a moment, possibly realizing how shallow her response had sounded since the pouty look had disappeared. "I guess…I hadn't thought of it like that. I guess I do care." In a more subdued voice, she said, "Help me mount, please? I've done some horseback riding with one of my old boyfriends, but I can't mount this giant horse without some help. May we leave now?"

"Och, in a hurry to leave me, aye?" He reached for her waist and tossed her up onto his horse before mounting behind her. He rode through the gate, waving to his ten guards to signal they should start their patrol. They would meet him later to report their findings.

"They aren't coming with us?"

"Nay, we're on my land. We willnae be bothered." Hellfire, but why did the lass have to smell so sweetly this morn? "Did ye take a bath or something? Why do ye smell like flowers?"

"I did. Jinty arranged for the tub to be brought to my room, I mean, chamber. And you look a bit cleaner than you did yesterday. Do you have a tub in your chamber?" she asked, glancing pointedly at his clean hair.

"Nay, but I did jump in the loch. It calms me when I get upset. Besides, tubs are for lasses," he replied. He had to admit he was curious about her time, if she indeed proved to be of sound mind. "Do ye bathe at home often?"

"Every day. We have showers. Hot water comes out of a spigot in the wall."

He tugged her hips back far enough that she had no choice but to lean against him. Before she left, he wished to smell her sweetness a wee bit longer. It was much better than the fragrance half his warriors emitted. "Out of the wall? How does it get there?"

"Lots of pipes. Don't ask. Only one of many modern conveniences we have that you don't."

They rode in silence for a while, his mind trying to imagine what her world was like, but he kept returning to how much he enjoyed her company.

A short time later, he asked, "So ye are anxious to return?" Why did he suddenly wish she would stay?

"Yes. I miss my sisters. I'm worried about them. May I ask you a question?"

"Aye, if I can answer, I will." His hand fell to her hip, the soft curve enticing him. He wished he dared to squeeze her there, but it wouldn't be wise. If the pool's magic sent her back to her time, she would leave forever. Besides which, his bollocks still ached from the memory of her blow. Instead, he tucked her backside just so until it was flush against him. She stilled, and he feared she'd push away, but she didn't, though she sat as straight as a board. "Go ahead," he prompted.

"What do you think happened to my sisters? Knowing it's a faerie pool and the one I jumped into probably was, too. Where do you think they are?"

"I think ye fell in the portal and they dinnae. They're probably still searching for ye in yer own time."

To his surprise, she fell back against him, probably so distracted she didn't realize what she'd done. But his loins couldn't help but respond to her curves rubbing against him in an erotic dance atop the horse, one that would beg him to do more if he knew her better.

He groaned before he could control it, and her reaction was swift as she sat up with a start. He could almost feel the blush spread across her body when she noticed his hardness.

"I think I'd prefer to walk."

He wasn't going to argue with her. Losing his erection would be quite a bit easier if he wasn't in contact with her. "Fine. We havenae far to go. But yer legs will tire."

She turned around to stare at him, her blush still visible. "Stop the horse. I'm getting down."

He did as she asked and helped her dismount from the horse. "As ye wish, lass. I apologize, but I cannae stop something when 'tis a natural occurrence out of my control."

She didn't speak but continued to walk forward, her head down. He couldn't believe she was still embarrassed or upset.

"Forgive me. I forget how innocent women are

who still have their maidenhead."

She stopped and whirled around to face him, staring up at him in a fury. "My maidenhead? I'm not a virgin. Where I come from, women can initiate the sex act. We aren't expected to hide our sexuality or control our desires."

Now *that* caught his interest. "Tell me more."

"We act on our desires as much as men do, and that's all you need to know. I'm not some innocent, but I didn't expect to have to deal with your dick just because I'm on your horse."

"My dick?"

"You know what I mean."

He certainly could guess, but then something he hated to see appeared out of nowhere—tears in the corners of her eyes. Och, tears again. But she turned around and began to head toward the pool again, not giving him the chance to comfort her.

He heard her mumbling even though she'd turned away from him. "What the hell have I gotten myself into? Dammit!"

"Ye truly do curse quite a bit for a lass."

"I'll curse as much as I like. Don't think you can bark orders at me the way you do your men. How much farther is it so I can get away from you?"

"We'll be there in less than an hour, but ye know there are many lassies here who wish for my attentions. Dinnae be so offended. 'Tis a compliment," he said with a chuckle.

She turned her head to narrow her gaze at him, but rather than swear at him again, she simply continued to walk away.

"Perhaps I better hurry." She took off at a run, heading into a meadow, sections of forest on both sides of her.

"Hellfire, but she's sensitive," he muttered under his breath as he flicked the reins of his horse to catch up to her. He was about to yell a warning, but it was too late.

Out of the woods came a snorting wild boar headed straight for her. She screamed and whirled around, running back toward him. Too far away to use his sword, he stopped his horse and pulled his bow from its spot on his back and nocked an arrow, ready to fire it at the wild pig. His heart raced when she stepped into his line of fire. What if he had accidentally let the arrow fly?

"Get down," he shouted.

Fortunately, his words registered and she fell to the ground, covering her head. He fired at the beast, killing him instantly, just as two more charged out of the woods. He took those two out easily. He pulled his horse up side of her and dismounted, his bow still in his hand. "Are ye all right, lass?"

"Yes. Are there more?" Her hands still covered her head in fear. The look on her face struck him right in his gut, but fortunately he'd caught the beasts before they could reach her.

"Stay there. I'll check the woods." He was glad they'd been boar instead of stags. Boar were slower, and their broad sides were easier to hit. He'd have his men take all three of them back to the keep. They'd eat well this week.

He ventured into the woods in two places, scouting for more boars, but didn't see any. Turning around, he headed back to where his horse was guarding Allison. She took him by surprise, launching herself at him and throwing her arms around his neck. Her babbling was near impossible for him to understand, but he did hear her thank him for his bravery.

He did something so out of character that he surprised himself.

He held her.

He hadn't held a woman in his arms of late, mostly because of the disaster with Shona, but also because he hadn't met a lass who stirred him—even Shona. He quite liked having his arms around Allison, taking in her sweet scent, feeling her ample curves molded against him, listening to her speak in her strange accent. Even her sharp tongue pleased him. The lass was a feisty woman, not easily intimidated, and he liked her that way.

When she finally fell quiet, he cupped her face and whispered, "I'm going tae kiss ye now, lass. If ye dinnae want me, push me away." He paused for a moment to give her the chance to refuse him, but she did not. His lips descended on hers, and instead of pushing him away, she tugged him closer, canting her head to give him better access to her delicious mouth. Her tongue darted out to taste his, and he couldn't stop himself from growling as he gripped her backside and lifted her up against him, his erection hitting her in just the right place.

She felt wonderful against him, better than any other woman ever had. Her hands were everywhere, gripping his biceps, finding his nipples and tweaking them, while he continued his assault on her mouth. Her sweet tongue teased him in such a way that he wished to devour her. He found a tree and leaned her up against it, freeing his hands to undo the ribbon on her gown and tug it down to expose her delectable breasts.

"Hell, but ye're beautiful," he whispered as he lowered his tongue to her nipple, bringing it to a taut peak. She moaned, thrusting against him. He reached underneath her skirts to find a barrier there, but she helped him push it down, grabbing him with her hand and leading him home. "Are ye sure ye want this? Because I've never wanted anyone as much as I want ye right now, but ye must agree with me, Allison."

"Yes, now. Yes, aye, whatever words you need, I want you inside me now."

It was the only invitation he needed. He lifted her and buried himself within her tight sheath with one thrust, a small roar coming from him when he met her slick juices. A delightful moan tore from the back of her throat, making him want her even more. Lowering his head to her breast, he took the mound full into his mouth, suckling her until she cried out. He didn't know if he could hold off, but the whimpering sounds she made nearly unmanned him, so he fought to bring her to climax first.

He swore he'd died and gone to heaven.

There was something about this lass that wouldn't let go.

CHAPTER EIGHT

ALLIE GRIPPED HIS HAIR, WANTING to finish this so badly she didn't care what he did to
her. When his mouth found her nipple, she nearly
screamed with pleasure, but she contained herself,
moving against him and urging him to go faster.

He pounded into her and he whispered, "Am I
hurting ye, lass?"

"Noooo," was all she could get out. "More,
please. Harder."

She was nearly there when he managed to move
one hand around and touch her clit, massaging her
until she climaxed with a shout, opening wider for
him. He buried himself inside her with a shout of
his own, finishing immediately after her.

When they finished, she clung to him, unable to
believe how she'd just acted. "Oh my God, I can't
believe…"

His forehead touched hers. "I dinnae plan that.
It just…yer bottom against me, yer lips, I couldnae help myself. Allison, 'twas unbelievable. Dinnae
blush so. I've never had a woman like that. I…"

He lowered her to the ground as though she were a fine piece of china about to break, after he'd pounded her hard enough to knock her halfway to China.

Allie couldn't stop the deep scarlet from crossing her face, her chest, everywhere. Her feet found the ground and her knees buckled, but he caught her.

"Easy, lass."

She was mortified that she'd acted so brazenly. She felt like a slut, but he'd made her feel gorgeous, special, more so than any of the other men she'd taken into her bed. Straightening her clothing, she stilled his hand when he tried to help her. "I don't normally… I've never been that fast…"

How could she explain to a medieval Highlander that she wasn't usually like this? They'd known each other for all of a day, and she'd spread her legs like a wanton and begged for more.

Without a condom.

"Oh my god, we didn't use anything. We didn't…" She paused, trying to remember when she'd last had her period, whether or not she would be fertile. No, probably not. She should get it shortly.

Then she chuckled, a nervous titter, but a laugh nonetheless.

Maybe this was a dream after all. How else could she explain this bit of wish fulfillment?

"Are ye all right? 'Twas most spectacular to me, but ye seem upset." He brushed his thumb down her cheek and across her jaw.

"No, never mind. You know, even if this is a dream, I'll remember *that*. I'll remember it for the rest of my life." He looked at her strangely, so she continued to ramble. When had she ever been handled so expertly? No man had ever massaged her clit as expertly as he had. She patted his shoulder and said, "Well done. You do know how to please a woman. Now, how far away is that faerie pool? Time for me to jump in so I can find my way home."

She stepped away from him and headed toward the faerie pool.

"Dinnae go." This was a man capable of a most alarming bellow, but the words came out in a quiet, almost subdued tone.

"What?" She turned around to see him standing not a foot away from her. His broad shoulders looked absolutely beautiful. The man was one hell of a specimen, all testosterone and muscle, grit and bravery. Braw, wasn't that how they said it in Scotland? Aye, he was one braw man, handsome as the devil with his one dimple and his ridiculous muscles.

"Dinnae leave me. Stay a few more days. Please." The stubble on his jaw called to her, begging her to run her hand across his face.

Stunned, she found herself verbalizing the first thought that popped into her mind. "Why?"

"Because I like ye. I care for ye, more than I've cared for any other lass in a verra long time."

She furrowed her brow. "Lachie told me you didn't love Shona, but didn't you have any feelings for her at all? You were supposed to marry her?"

Those delicious shoulders slumped. "Aye, but 'twas a match made by my sire with our allies. 'Twas no' our choice. Her choice was to leave me. Just like my sire and my mother, my betrothed left me and my brother chose another over me. Stay until Lachie returns. Please. I'd like to know more about ye."

Something throbbed deep inside her. She knew exactly how he felt. Everyone he'd cared for had deserted him. Her parents were gone, too, and she'd lost her sisters. No, they hadn't left her on purpose, but they'd still left.

She whispered, "I'm sorry, but I can't. I have to go back."

He nodded, his face turning to stone, the small bit of vulnerability disappearing from his expression. "Do as ye must. 'Tis through those trees there."

She nodded, then grabbed him and gave him a quick kiss that was not returned. She said, "Thank you for everything. Will you wait until I'm gone so the pigs don't attack me again?"

"They're boars, not pigs. But aye, I'll give ye half the hour." He didn't look at her as he said it, but perhaps that was as it should be. No regrets.

She took the bundle of her things, then ran through the trees and into the clearing around the faerie pool. The grass had turned into a fine moss, with flowers climbing up the rocks toward the back of the pool. The water was as still as could be.

She changed into her old clothing, leaving the borrowed gown on one of the rocks, then climbed into the water, surprised to find it so warm. On her last visit, she'd been too out of sorts to notice anything other than that her surroundings had changed dramatically.

The bottom of the pool was all rock, a bit slippery, so she found her way to the middle, turning around to see if he'd followed her.

He wasn't there.

Stepping into the water hadn't caused her to disappear, but why she thought it would work, she didn't know. She'd gotten here through a waterfall, and this was simply a pool. Maybe she'd have to submerge herself. She dropped to her knees and the water rose to shoulder level. Holding her breath, she attempted to dip her head underneath the surface.

She couldn't do it.

He'd asked her to stay. A fine, honorable, sinfully hot Highlander had asked her to stay because he liked her.

What was wrong with her? Even her sisters would call her foolish if they knew the full situation. After all the cheating boyfriends she'd endured, she knew they would approve of Brann. Despite the centuries that should have stood between them, she felt she could be herself around him—more so than with anyone she'd ever dated before.

She dipped back down, but she stood up again before the water could rise over her chin.

Her mind was playing games with her.

He'd asked her to stay until Lachie returned. What would it hurt if she stayed for a few more days?

She could make sure Smoky was not tossed away as the runt of the litter. They could have hot sex three more times because she had those condoms in the keep.

Allie kneaded her forehead as she stood in the pool, basking in the warmth of the water, nearly moaning at how good it felt, or was she moaning from the memory of how good it had felt to be held in such strong arms? To be pleasured by a man who was as close to a god as anyone she'd ever met.

Tipping her head back, she sighed as a surge of heat warmed her insides again, much like that brusque Highlander had heated every inch of her.

She climbed out of the pool, reached for the dry gown, then jumped when the man she'd just been fantasizing about stepped into the clearing.

"It didn't work, lass?"

She smiled. "I don't know. I changed my mind. Decided I could wait a few days, if the offer is still open."

He ambled over to stand in front of her, the slight upturn of his lips spreading into a warm smile. "It is." His hand reached up to cup her cheek, his thumb rubbing the skin near her mouth, a sensuous caress that nearly caused her to moan.

"Will you come back with me when I'm ready to try again?" Suddenly lost in the depth of his green eyes, she was powerless to turn him down, even if he refused to return with her.

Maybe it wasn't just him. Maybe she wanted to explore the area—or rather, era—a bit more. If she returned, she may never be able to get back to this time period again. This could be her only chance.

"I will," he said.

She let out a breath she hadn't realized she'd been holding, then briefly touched her tongue to his thumb. "There's only one other condition."

"What?"

"You have to use a condom the next time we have sex. Three times—that's all you get. And please turn your back so I can dress."

"But I've already tasted ye…"

She gave his shoulder a shove. "Please?"

He chuckled but gave her his back. "I agree to yer terms, but what the hell is a condom?"

Even though he couldn't see her, she had to smile.

"I'll show you later what a condom does," she whispered.

CHAPTER NINE

BRANN TURNED HIS HEAD TOWARD the sound of horses. "Lass, ye best hurry. My men are nearly here."

She squealed and tossed her wet clothes into a heap, throwing the gown over her shoulders in mere seconds.

And not a moment too soon. The urgency of his men's approach told him something was amiss, an impression that was confirmed when they came into view. These were not the men he'd sent on patrol. "What is it?"

His second, Angus, replied, "The Sinclair is almost on our land."

He spun around to see if Allison was fully covered. "'Tis nae time to be shy, lass. Sinclair is our rival. I must see what he wants, and I ne'er trust him."

"I'm dressed," she said in a whisper, casting a pointed look toward Angus.

Later he'd explain to her that Angus would never betray him or say anything about finding them together. He took her hand and moved closer to Angus. "What does he want? Have ye heard anything?"

"Naught. No clue."

"How many are there?"

"Two dozen. No' a fighting number. He carries his banner, so he appears to be here in peace, but ye're right no' to trust him. Mayhap ye should send her back to the castle with some of the men. Ye know how ruthless Clan Sinclair can be with lasses."

"Nay. She'll stay with me for that verra reason. I'll meet him with ye. Find our men. The ones patrolling the area. We shall catch up with Clan Sinclair by the time they reach our land."

He released Allison's hand, then lowered his hand to the small of her back and ushered her toward his horse just as several more of his men joined them. He let Angus give instructions to the men while he devoted his full attention to Allison. She had to understand the potential danger of the situation they were about to enter. He didn't know for sure what the Sinclair had in mind, but he was certain he did not trust him.

"We need to mount and get moving," he said. "Ye'd be wise no' to speak to anyone from Clan Sinclair. Angus speaks the truth. They're no' to be trusted." When they reached his mount, he lifted her up onto his horse's back, stifling a groan as Allison's scent wafted past him. Their interlude had been sweet, but he needed to focus. Her life could depend on it. Clan Sinclair stole women all the time. It was their favorite pastime.

Angus led the way while his men surrounded

him, as they were trained to do for their chieftain. Brann had move to the front when they were certain it was safe. As soon as they caught sight of the Sinclair group, he slowed his horse so he could repeat his warning, wanting to be certain she understood the danger. "Please remember what I said about them. And do no' stare at any of them. They'll think it gives them the right to take ye."

"Take me? You are kidding, right?"

"I dinnae understand…"

"Jesting. You're jesting about one of them taking me, right?" The doubt in her eyes turned to fear when he didn't answer her right away.

"Sometimes 'tis the way of the Highlands. Warriors steal their brides. But dinnae worry yerself—'tis my job to protect ye." He rubbed his hand along the side of her hip, wishing he could take the time to know every part of her body.

He would before she went back.

He whistled and the Sinclair group stopped their horses. Angus and several of his own men rode up on either side and behind him as protection, if necessary, but he doubted Sinclair was here to cause trouble. He didn't have enough men.

The two groups faced off. "Sinclair, what brings ye to MacKay land?"

The laird of Clan Sinclair, Wallas Sinclair, grinned, a look Brann did not trust. "We've come in peace. I've brought some of our best wine to share with ye. A gift from our clan to yers."

"Why?" Brann wasn't fooled. Sinclair had an ulterior motive for certain. He always did.

"I have a proposal for ye, but I'd like to speak in private. May we meet in yer solar, Laird?" He tipped his head, but then his gaze found Allison. He ran his eyes down the length of her and back up again in a way that made Brann want to run him through with his sword.

"We'll meet in my solar," he said out of gritted teeth. "Ye have one hour to tell me what ye wish. Then I'll send ye on yer way."

"Is this the lass who bested ye at the corners? I heard she dropped ye to yer knees. I wish I'd been there myself, but alas, I was no'," Wallas Sinclair said, snickering. A couple of his men behind him chuckled and waggled their brows at her.

"Dinnae look at them. I'm warning ye," he whispered in her ear. He could feel her bristling behind him, but this was no time for her sauciness, as much as he loved that part of her.

"Is she taken?" Sinclair asked. "If not, I'll take her."

Brann set his hand on her hip, staking his claim, before he said, "She's taken."

"By whom?"

"By me. And ye'll stop staring at her."

"I'll buy her from ye. She looks like a wee wild-cat."

"She's no' for sale."

Brann could almost feel the fury rise from her toes up to her chest before it burst from her mouth. He squeezed her hip in another attempt to silence her, but it did no good.

"You want to buy me? Who the hell buys women, you pig? I'm not for sale and no one owns me."

"Allison, keep quiet."

"Don't tell me what to do, either of you. I know you all have a strange view of women, but I'll not be owned or bought by anyone. Do you hear me?"

Brann closed his eyes briefly as the entire group of Sinclair warriors burst into laughter.

Wallas Sinclair held his hand up to quiet them, and they stilled instantly. He moved his horse a few steps closer. "A strong woman. A strong, feisty woman. Where are ye from, lass? Ye talk strange, even for an English." His gaze bore into hers. "I want her. Name yer price, MacKay."

For some strange reason, Allison closed her mouth this time. She leaned back against him, but he could tell she was on the verge of screaming or bursting into tears. He hoped she'd scream.

"She's no' for sale. She's mine. If ye wish to talk, ye've cut yer time to a quarter hour. Follow me to my keep. Ye're to come in quickly and only with yer second."

Sinclair finally pulled his gaze from Allison and nodded. "Understood."

Brann hoped he wouldn't regret this move. He had a bad feeling about this.

A really bad feeling.

CHAPTER TEN

BRANN BROUGHT HIS HORSE TO a can-
ter as they headed back toward his keep. His
warriors stayed behind them as protection, the
Sinclair warriors behind them. No words were
bantered about between the two groups—Scottish
clan warriors weren't normally friendly with one
another unless they were at the corners competing.
Then the banter was mostly boasting and taunting.

Allison said, "I'm sorry, but I couldn't help
myself."

"I warned ye that if ye looked at them, they'd try
to steal ye."

"How can he steal a woman? Is that really allowed
in this time? People are arrested and imprisoned
for kidnapping where I'm from."

"'Tis done frequently. Men steal women for
wives. However, he willnae try to steal ye since
I've spoken for ye. But please, lass, mind yer tongue.
Lasses are nae so bold in this time. I admire it in ye,
but ye must tread with care."

"I should have gone back. Nothing will keep

me here." The tears in her voice vexed him more than the kick she'd delivered to his bollocks the day before.

He leaned closer to whisper in her ear. "Ye promised me a few days. Please dinnae change yer mind. I promise ye better times once I send them off. I need ye by my side." How could he convince her to stay? "Mind ye, we dinnae even know if ye will be able to go back for certes. I hate to see ye get yer hopes up for something that willnae work."

"Well, it should work," she mumbled under her breath.

"Aye, but it may no'. Other people swim in the pool. Ye arenae the only one. They dinnae disappear."

She turned around to stare at him, those blasted tears misting her eyes again.

"I promise to help ye. If nae that way, there may be another." He gave her a soft squeeze, something he enjoyed way too much.

She leaned back against him, and he kissed her neck ever so briefly. He thought he heard her sniffle. He'd rather bear the brunt of her sharp tongue than hear her cry.

They arrived at the gate, and he instructed his guards to allow only Wallas Sinclair and his second inside the gate. The rest would wait outside. After he dismounted and helped Allison do the same, he waited for Sinclair and his second to arrive.

Rather than offer any sort of greeting, he simply nodded to them and led the way into the keep, his hand on the small of Allison's back.

Brann motioned to Jinty as soon as they stepped through the door and she hurried over. "Aye, my lord?"

"Have the serving lasses bring a platter of cheeses and meat pies to the solar, Jinty. We'll no' be long." He did not request wine because Sinclair had brought his bottle. The maid nodded and left. He motioned for Allison to precede him into the solar, and the unwelcome visitors followed her in before he and Angus did the same.

Sinclair raised his brows. "Ye'll allow a female to join our discussion?"

"Aye," Brann replied, his gaze telling all he would not bend on the issue. "If ye dinnae like it, take yer leave now. She stays by my side."

Sinclair made a noise indicating his displeasure with the situation, but sat down in front of Brann's desk. Angus had brought goblets in and poured wine for all.

"I just returned from Edinburgh and brought it with me," Sinclair said, tasting the wine first. "I'm sure ye'll enjoy it."

"I have nae time for small talk. Get to yer point, Sinclair. We've no' been friendly before. Why the sudden change?" He pulled an extra chair over to his desk and sat down when she did.

"As ye wish. I've heard ye arenae on good terms with Taran and he lives on the part of yer land that borders mine."

"Aye, 'twas a gift from me to Taran and his new wife. Why do ye care?"

"I'd like to propose an alliance. Murray has his sights set on my land, but ye and I could take his clan over together."

"I have no problems with Clan Murray. What of yers?" Brann didn't like the way this conversation was going. Ewan Murray had been a friend to Brann and Taran ever since they were young. They were all near the same age, and they had been the very best of friends, so close that Ewan's sire had died within six months of his sire. He and the Murray held an alliance of sorts, though it did not go much further than a mutual agreement not to attack each other. It was the kind of alliance he understood.

Any other kind of alliance, he didn't trust—just like he did not trust Sinclair.

"I'll be honest with ye, and ye best listen and get off yer high horse, MacKay. I've discovered that the Murray is wanting to join yer brother to attack ye. He thinks the two of ye are sorely divided and ye are ripe for the overtake. If he bests ye and yer brother both because the two of ye are lovesick over a pair of thighs, ye'll lose everything. I'm suggesting we work together and overtake Murray when he comes at ye. Ye'll need my help because he's built his force up to near two hundred. How many have ye?"

"Ye want to form an alliance with me because Murray plans to join forces with my brother and attack us?" He fought the urge to snort at the older man. Little did he know Brann had built his number of warriors to over three hundred, but it would be a tactical mistake to give that information out. He had some men on patrols and others in the lists. Sinclair would not be able to guess his numbers from such a short visit.

"Aye, 'struth and ye need to consider it. Dinnae waste time. He plans to attack in a fortnight as he has more men coming."

Brann muddled over this information, unsure of his best plan of action. He did not at all believe Sinclair, but rejecting him so quickly may not be the correct course. Perhaps he could get to Murray and see what he had to say about Sinclair, act as though he'd only heard tales from traveling minstrels. He wouldn't talk with Taran unless he had no choice.

He had a sennight to make up his mind, though he thought it best to agree with the man at the moment. Brann had not made many friends of late.

"Och, what'll it be, MacKay? I havenae the time to wait all day for yer agreement. If ye dinnae agree, I'll find another." He stood up, knocking his chair backward, motioning to his second that it was time for them to take their leave.

"Hold yerself. I accept yer proposal, Sinclair."

"Fine." The laird picked up his goblet of wine and held it up. "To our new alliance."

"To our new alliance." He said nothing else, not wanting to give Sinclair too much information.

They drank to the agreement, but the atmosphere was still tense. They'd been rivals too long for either of them to accept this agreement with joy.

Allison couldn't help but think she'd made a huge mistake. Agreeing to stay to satisfy her own sexual needs had not been smart. Navigating this culture she'd been thrown into was paramount to her survival, so she vowed to hold her tongue in the future.

Angus left to escort the Sinclair and his second out of the castle, but Brann motioned for her to stay inside the solar, so she moved to a chair across from his desk and sat down. Once the door closed, he kneaded his forehead and sighed, something that told her he had no idea what to do with her. She gave him the chance to gather his thoughts, because she was quite sure a lecture was in store for her.

She'd listen, agree with him, have hot sex three times tonight, and then leave tomorrow. She'd always wondered if she were multi-orgasmic.

Curbing her impulse to snicker, she coughed so she could put her hand in front of her mouth.

If only her sisters could see her now.

He sat down in front of her instead of returning to the seat behind his desk and rested his elbows on his knees. "If what my sire told me is true, if ye really are some type of faerie who came through the portal, then I cannae imagine how confused ye must be, but ye must learn to trust me. 'Tis my job as chief to protect ye, but I also feel 'tis my job as my sire's son to protect ye as he did my mother. Can I ask ye to trust me, lass? I dinnae know if ye've noticed the swords we carry, but spouting off at me enemy could get us into a heap of trouble. And rest assured that he is my enemy. He'll only be my friend so long as it suits his needs, and I'm no' even certain I believe anything he just said."

"I know. My world is so different. We've just gone through this entire movement meant to empower women, and I…" How could she possibly explain the rise of the female voice to this man? "Forgive me, Brann. I'll remember to stay silent. I didn't like the way they stared at me, I didn't… Never mind. It isn't important. I understand your point, and I'll do my best not to cause any issues in the future."

He helped her to her feet, and to her surprise, he cupped her face and kissed her, one of the sweetest kisses she'd ever experienced, so much so that she whimpered when he pulled back. He quirked his brow at her, a crooked smile on his face as he chucked her under her chin.

She turned her face to hide her blush. What was she to do when the man kissed her as though she were the most treasured person on the planet? That had never happened to her before. Well, maybe the kiss that nerd had given her in middle school, but that kiss hadn't left her feeling like she were the finest piece of chocolate.

It had been more like being dipped in a vat of saliva because the boy had been a bit excited.

A knock at the door interrupted her thoughts, and it opened to reveal Angus with an awful expression on his face.

"What is it?" Brann asked his second.

"The Murray is nearly here, my lord."

Allison had her suspicions about what this could entail, and she guessed it wasn't going to be good. The look of concern on Brann's face told her everything, so she decided to take the initiative to get the hell out of there. "I think I'll go to the kitchens to find my puppy."

"Stay there?" Brann suggested, his brow arched in question.

"Yes, I'll stay out of the way. I promise." She hustled away, but Brann was right behind her, his hand at the small of her back. He gave her one final caress as he left with Angus. Why did that one small touch mean more than anything her latest ex had ever done?

She hurried out the back door of the keep so she'd not be seen by the newcomers, but as soon as she stepped out back, a pair of strong arms grabbed her from behind and clinched her tight against his body.

So shocked to have been accosted so, she didn't respond at first. It was only after he spun her around and she found herself facing a man wearing a strange plaid that she sprang into action. She kicked the unsuspecting man square in his balls and he dropped in front of her, grabbing and covering his privates as if she'd attack him again.

She glanced around but saw no one else.

That set her into a fury. She bent over and grabbed him by the neck, squeezing it in just the right places to cause him serious trouble while she leaned one knee toward his balls. This particular hold could cause the man to have a stroke. That wasn't her goal, but she *did* wish to scare the hell out of him.

She tightened her grip as she bent closer to deliver her warning. "Do not ever touch me again."

He stared at her in incomprehension, so she squeezed even tighter. "Do you understand me?"

He nodded, his eyes unable to stay focused on her because he was losing the blood flow to his head. His mumbling was incomprehensible to her, and she didn't even try to decipher it. They were probably Gaelic curse words.

She let go, spinning on her heel and stalking off toward the kitchens, unable to think about what might have happened until she stepped inside. She leaned against the wall and took a deep breath, searching the area for her little puppy.

The trembling began, just as it always did after a stressful event. She heard the mewling sounds of dear Smoky and found the pup's crate in the corner. Jinty had kept her promise.

"Hello, sweet pea. How are you doing?" Smoky's tail wagged, so Allie picked her up, hoping the animal would settle the nerves in her belly. "Are you hungry?"

She stepped into the main area in search of Cook, carrying the puppy and her crate with her. "Cook? I'm taking Smoky."

Cook's gruff voice answered her a moment later. "Fine. She dinnae eat much for me. Mayhap ye should feed her. There's fresh goat's milk in the urn."

"Thank you, Cook. I'll see you later."

She heard another grunt from the woman. Maybe grunts were all she could manage after spending the entire day in this infernal heat. Smoky yipped at her, turning her little face up to her as if to remind her of her existence.

"I'll no' forget you." She was starting to talk like the rest of them. "I mean, I won't forget you." Locating the milk, she poured some into a bowl, grabbed some clean linen squares, and stepped out into the cool air, but not before she peeked out to make sure the coast was clear of that bastard from Clan Sinclair.

He was gone, so she made her way to the keep, but then decided to set Smoky down in the grass to see to her needs. Moving over toward the stone wall, she found a small area of soft grass and moss for Smoky and then set the puppy down so she could commence her sniffing routine.

The waterworks began as soon as she sat down. How could someone have thought it was okay to just grab her like that? What made men so foolish? Other than Brann and the hot sex, was there any other reason for her to stay in a time period where women were treated like commodities?

No. None.

As the deluge of tears covered her face, she vowed to end this.

One night of hot sex and then off to the faerie pool.

CHAPTER ELEVEN

E WAN MURRAY SAT IN BRANN'S solar.
"And do ye care to tell me why the bastard
Sinclair was leaving here? I saw him, and I'll tell
ye he was smirking about something. What happened?"

"Smirking? I gave him no reason to smirk, Murray, but I dinnae need to tell ye all we discussed.
He's concerned ye are aiming for his lands. That
ye've joined with my brother to take over his and
my land. 'Struth?"

Murray appeared genuinely confused. "Nay.
'Tis no' true. I swear it. I'd never collude agin ye
Brann, on my sire's honor. Ye know how close our
sires were. My sire would roll over in his grave if
he thought I was planning agin ye. I've talked to
Taran, but only about your differences. I came to
tell ye how happy he and Shona are."

"I dinnae care to hear about my brother's happiness. He's nae brother of mine. He made his
choice."

"Brann, I understand your pride, but ye must get

past it. If for nae other reason than Lachie. Ye cannae wish for him to take sides. The two of ye are stronger together than apart. If what ye say about Sinclair is true, look how quickly he moved to take advantage of your animosity toward each other."

Brann snorted, knowing full well that Murray spoke the truth about him and Taran, but how was he to accept it? He could not. His wounded pride would not allow it. He would rather die than admit it, but it was his brother's abandonment that hurt far worse than Shona's.

"I'll no' make Lachie choose. He's just a laddie, and one who had to grow up without his parents. But I cannae join with Taran again."

"Ye'll no' go for the land ye gave him, will ye? Ye'll be honorable, will ye no'? He's yer brother, Brann. Ye cannae go agin him or yer sire will haunt ye. And probably mine, too."

Brann couldn't help but grin at that. Ewan's sire had been a crusty old goat, but with a heart as big as the sun. "Nay, yer sire would scare me if he haunted me." He crossed his ankles and set them up on his desk, leaning back in his chair. "I'll no' fight my own brother, but I'll nae longer aid him either. I prefer to ignore him. He can live his life as he sees fit so long as he stays away."

"Does it hurt ye so much to see him with Shona?"

Brann scowled and chuckled. "Nay. I ne'er had any strong feelings for Shona."

Now that he knew what it felt like to be truly besotted with a lass, he was even more certain he had no feelings for Shona. But Allison? She would haunt his dreams for many nights after she left him.

"What is it?" Ewan asked.

"What?"

"Ye have a wistful look on yer face. If no' for Shona, then who?"

He dropped his feet to the floor, his boots hitting the stone with a resounding thump. "No' Shona. 'Tis all ye need to know."

"My advice to ye is to find another wife and rejoin yer brother. Ye'll all be the better for it. Shall I send one of our lasses to ye?"

"Nay. I'm no' quite ready for that yet." He wouldn't tell him that he had plans for a sweet lass with an even sweeter arse.

"So Sinclair wants to go agin me? Is that what ye said?" Murray pressed.

"Aye. Ye know I'll no' do it, but I dinnae trust him. I had to agree to get him away from here. I dinnae want him planning agin me. Papa always taught me to know yer enemies." And to get him away from Allison. He didn't like the way the man looked at her. In fact, he wondered where she was at the moment. Had it been a mistake to send her away on her own?

"As long as ye dinnae carry out yer promise. I'll no' speak with Taran of this, but if ye change yer mind about wanting a sweet lass, I have a couple in mind. Ye seem preoccupied about something today, so I'll take my leave. I brought a cask of my best ale for ye."

"Many thanks, Murray. Have ye heard anything from MacDonnell?" He didn't wish to ask after Shona's sire, but the man could turn enemy as fast as any other.

"Nay. He's lying low. I heard he was sick, heaving all the time, so I've stayed away. I doubt he'll be out until he feels this shaming over ye and Shona is over. I'll take my leave. Make sure ye advise me of the Sinclair's plans. Ye're welcome at my keep anytime."

"My thanks to ye," he said as he clasped Ewan on the back. "I'll walk out with ye, mayhap ride with ye for a bit. I'd like to make sure the lout is off my land and no' wandering around."

As they made their way to the stables, Brann's gaze scanned the courtyard, looking for a lass with long legs and golden hair. He didn't see her, but he tried not to worry. Maybe she was inside the keep with the puppy.

He mounted his horse and followed the Murray out, surprised to see a couple of his men just returning from a patrol. They weren't due back for some time.

"Chief, may we speak with ye?" His men knew better than to disclose important information around another chieftain.

He waved to Ewan and said, "I'll keep ye abreast of all that transpires."

Ewan nodded. "I'll have my man leave the cask on the steps to yer hall."

"Many thanks." Brann led his men off to the side, far enough away from Ewan's men to guarantee privacy.

"What has ye concerned?" Brann asked, looking from one guard to the other.

"Just something unusual. We headed out but then circled back because I thought I saw something. We saw one Sinclair guard leaving by himself. And he appeared to be coming from the back of the castle. Thought ye should know, Chief."

"Ye mean he was coming from behind the castle? Do ye think he came out the back entrance?" Brann was mystified. Why would a Sinclair be at the back of his castle?

"Aye, we asked him what he was doing, but he sped off. Looked as if he was in great pain."

Some odd bit of intuition made him ask the next question. "Thank ye for the information. Have ye seen Allison about?"

One guard looked to the other before they shook their heads in unison. "She's not out on yer land, Chief."

Brann had a suspicion he couldn't erase.

It was time to find Allison.

Allison finally forced herself to stop crying. There was no reason to make such a fuss. Wouldn't it be better to enjoy the time she had left?

Her stomach reminded her that it was time to eat, so she headed toward the hall, carrying Smoky in the crook of her arm, the dog's favorite place.

"Sweet Smoky, I hate to think what could have happened," she whispered, kissing the puppy's head. "What if that man had caught me and tried to steal me away? Then Brann would have chased after him and impaled the bastard on his sword, just like any knight would do…" She couldn't help but stare off into space as she walked across the back part of the keep to the door. Back home, she'd wished for a man like the heroes in Jennae Vale's novels. One who was strong and honorable, who'd always protect her, and who'd make her orgasm before he did.

Hmmm…kind of like Brann. Maybe she *should* stay longer.

Then again, had the worst happened, Brann would probably have murdered the brute defending her honor. Were there consequences for murder in the 1300s? How the hell would she know?

She'd hated history in high school and had never taken it again.

"Smoky, I'm sorry to tell you this, but I'm an odd number in an even-numbered world. I don't belong here, so it's probably best for me to go back. The longer I wait, the more likely it is that my sisters will give up on me."

Smoky whined, licking her arm.

"Don't try to soften me up. Lachie will take care of you, and I'll make Brann promise to help him."

The sudden memory of that rotten bastard's hands on her gave her a chill that traveled up her spine. He had no right, even in these times. Brann had told the chief she was spoken for.

"Don't look at me like that, Smoky. I can't stay here. I'd have nothing to do but take care of you and have hot sex with Brann." At least she was needed back in present time. There was such a shortage of nurses she'd *always* be needed.

But she didn't like her job. In her previous job, she'd pulled brutal twelve-hour shifts at a hospital. Every night she'd be so exhausted she'd just lie in bed, unable to sleep, thinking about all the things she hadn't been able to get to during her shift. The nice things she would have liked to do for the patients.

So she'd left that job to take a position at a dermatology office. The working conditions were great, but it was hard to feel rewarded helping the doctor hand out medicines for acne and removing basal cell cancers.

She'd been in a quandary for the last three months. She wanted to matter, but she didn't want to take years off her life helping others.

Smoky yipped as if to move her along.

"Fine, we'll go in. I know you're just hoping for some meat, but you're too young." Once inside, she made a beeline to the hearth and set the crate down. She arranged the blanket inside and set Smoky down on top of it. The wee pup circled three times, nuzzling the blanket with her nose, before she found the perfect position and lay down, closing her eyes with a deep sigh of contentment.

"I've tired you out with all my talking." She petted the pup's head and then stood up, looking for a place to wash her hands.

That wasn't going to happen. Maybe she should start carrying her hand sanitizer. She found a small pitcher of water on a side table and poured a bit over her hands, rubbing them together before cascading another few drops over her fingers.

"They dinnae look dirty." Brann strode up, a smile on his face.

"No, but they are. I wish you had soap around."

"I have a sliver in my sporran. Would ye like it?"

"No, I'll be fine."

"Would ye share the meal with me?" he asked.

"I'd love to." She followed him over to the dais, newly aware of all the men following their progress. He guided her onto a platform at the end of the hall. The long table and chairs on top faced the trestle tables full of guards, some wives, and local clan members.

"Thank you," she said, sitting in the chair Brann offered.

She hadn't been there long when a serving girl came over with an odd-looking bowl filled with a type of stew.

Brann ignored the girl's stare and said, "Bridget, see that someone opens the cask of ale that Murray brought. I'll have some of that."

She brought over two goblets filled with the ale. Allie briefly touched her tongue to the liquid, turned her nose up, and then shook her head. "No, thank you. I'll have water, please."

Brann laughed at her but took the ale, drinking half of it down. He then waved to his men, many of whom got up to get their own drink.

"So, lass. Other than yer sisters, what do ye miss most from yer land?" He took his dagger out of his pocket and stuck it into the bowl in front of him, cutting off a piece of it and dipping it into the stew.

"That's bread?"

"Aye, ye've not seen it before?"

"Well, I've seen something similar…" She'd seen bread bowls before, but this bread was quite dark and much coarser than she was used to eating. "You don't use many dishes, do you?" In truth, they wouldn't be practical here, especially without a dishwasher or a sink. "Anyway, that doesn't matter. You asked me a question, and I'd have to say the cleanliness is what I miss most."

"Jinty keeps a clean hall. Dinnae let her hear ye say otherwise, or she'll be blistering yer ear all night," he said, a most serious expression on his face.

"I see…I understand…How can I…" She had to think carefully about what she was about to say. "Many years from now, scientists learned about microbes."

He stared at her blankly.

"There are millions of little germs everywhere." She couldn't quite decide how to teach the man about the basics of microbiology. Germs and microbes were probably not the best way to start.

"What in blazes is a germ?"

She decided to change tactics. "You recall how I told you about the way we bathe? The spigot in the wall?"

"Aye, I like such a suggestion."

"Well, we have running water everywhere. The pipes bring water to different places in a building. In the kitchens, you would have a big wide bowl with faucets or spigots at the top that release water. Cook would be able to cook with the water and use it for dishes."

"It brings it right from the well?"

"Something like that." She decided explaining about toilets would be too difficult. "And we have giant tubs with spigots for washing clothes."

His eyes widened. "That could be verra useful. But when ye're done, how do ye get the water back out? Ye have to carry it in tubs and dump it?"

"No, we have drains that bring the water to pipes that take it back out."

"Impressive. So everything is cleaner. 'Tis truly what you miss?"

"Yes. I could wash my hands whenever I wanted, or wash the table, or…"

"Wash the table? Why the devil would ye need to wash the table? Crumbs just brush off."

Allie looked at the beautifully carved table in front of them, much nicer than the trestle tables below them. There were knife marks and scratches galore, but it was still quite lovely. But how often had it been washed?

Had it *ever* been washed?

A maid brought over a bowl with water in it.

"What do you use that for?" she asked, afraid to use it for what she wished.

He smirked. "We're no' so dirty. 'Tis for washing yer fingers after ye eat from the trencher."

She glanced around the room, but no one else had a bowl of water.

"She brought it for ye, lass. Females are a wee bit fussier than men."

"How thoughtful of her." She used it right away, wondering how they didn't all die from food poisoning. "Where do you keep your food?"

"Some things in the kitchen, others in the pantry, the larder, or the buttery."

"Oh, you must have lots of butter if you have a larder and a buttery."

His brow furrowed the way it always did when she unintentionally said something dense. "Butter? The buttery holds the ale butts or barrels. 'Tis what makes it a buttery, lass."

"No iceboxes?" She knew they didn't have refrigerators, but how did they keep everything fresh?

"Ice? 'Tis summer. There's no ice in the lochs this time of year. We have an icehouse in the winter, but where would we get the ice now?" He gave her a strange look, so she decided maybe it was best to change the subject.

If she thought any more about germs and cleanliness, she'd be up in her room crying.

CHAPTER TWELVE

BRANN HAD TORTURED HIMSELF LONG enough. She'd asked for a bath but had changed her mind upon being reminded she'd just come from the faerie pool. Still, she'd grabbed an ewer of fresh water before disappearing upstairs for some time alone. He'd thought she would come back down to the great hall to invite him to her chamber, but he hadn't seen her yet.

His loins had waited long enough.

"What do ye wish me to do with them on the morrow?" Angus asked.

"What?" He truly had no idea what the man was talking about.

"The morrow?"

He couldn't stay away from her any longer.

"Ye're a bit agitated, my lord," Jinty said as she cleaned up the tables, keeping a wide berth between herself and Brann.

"So I am. Do as ye wish, Angus. I'm going to my bed." He stomped across the hall and up the staircase, ignoring all the stares. He bet they'd have much to say as soon as he was gone.

Did they think he liked the pull the lass had on him? She'd be the death of him yet with those big blue eyes and pouty lips.

This time, she'd beg him for more. He couldn't help but smile at the memory of the lass's screams of pleasure. They could have been heard on Murray land. His chest puffed out a bit as he sauntered over to her door.

"Come in," she said as soon as he knocked. Her voice was low and sultry.

He opened the door and peeked around the corner, surprised to see her sprawled across the bed on her side, the curve of her hip begging for his tongue. Her head was propped on her hand, her bent elbow leaning against the bed.

She was naked as the day of her birth, and more glorious than any woman he'd ever seen.

"Lass, ye leave me speechless." He stood next to the bed, taking in the view of her, his erection lifting his plaid until he unhooked his brooch and tossed it off to the side. He kicked off his boots and his woolen socks, and lowered himself on the bed next to her, the covers already pulled back and waiting for him. "Ye are as beautiful as they come."

His eyes traveled from her face down to her toes. "I guess ye couldnae have come down to fetch me looking like that." As he stared down at her, admiring every inch, she lifted her free hand and shook a small packet back and forth. He waggled his eyebrows at her, his wide grin telling her how much he enjoyed her nudity. "What have ye there, Allison?" He grinned, lying flat on his back, his hands clasped behind his head.

"A condom."

"A what?"

"Something a man puts on to keep a woman from getting preg—I mean, with child."

As soon as her comment hit home, he yanked his hands out from behind his head and covered his private area, his erection leaving him as quickly as it had come. "And why would I wish to put something on myself? I like it the way it is."

"A condom. Remember how I said I wanted you to wear this? I have three of them."

He took the flimsy package and brought it up close so he could study it. "How does it work?"

"I'll place it on your penis and roll the edges down carefully over it, and you won't even know it's there."

"A dick cover? Ye wish for me to cover my dick so I cannot have my release? 'Tis no' sounding appealing to me."

She burst out laughing. "A dick cover? I like that. I guess you could call it that, but it won't affect your release. It's quite thin."

He stared at the package again and said, "It willnae fit. 'Tis too small." He handed it back to her with this pronouncement, dismissing the issue.

"Says every man on the planet and you're all wrong. It will fit fine. See." She held it up for him to see. "Extra large. I guessed Scottish men would be bigger than American men." She tore the package open for his inspection.

"Look at the size of the ring. It'll never fit. I'll no' allow ye to put it on me."

"No?" she asked with a saucy grin. "We'll see."

Her lips captured his, and she swept her tongue

inside his mouth before he could even react. He took over and plundered her mouth, dueling tongues with her, while his hands found her breasts and teased her nipples to taut peaks that he wished to taste.

He ended the kiss and rolled her underneath him, trailing his tongue between the valley of her breasts and up to her nipples, suckling each one until she cried out. She bucked her hips against him, but he didn't let her take over, instead taking his tongue down the middle of her belly to the juncture between her thighs. He licked and suckled until she cried out, going over the edge so quickly he couldn't help but smile with pride.

When she could finally speak again, she whispered, "Not fair," gasping between each word.

He chuckled as she maneuvered him onto his back, but the laughter didn't last long when she proceeded to do the same thing to him, trailing kisses down his chest and running the edge of her teeth over each nipple. He gripped her hips and tried to move her above him, but she managed to squeeze out, "Not yet…"

He groaned as her hands roamed over his body, finally gripping his manhood and milking him with a slow, rhythmic movement that was sheer torture. Then her tongue moved to the head of his penis, and he nearly shouted, but he stopped as he watched her perform the most erotic dance he'd ever seen. She teased him by dragging her tongue up the entire length of him before taking his full length in her mouth. He closed his eyes for a moment to savor the feelings she evoked, and when he opened them again, she was slipping something down the length of him.

He tried to bolt off the bed, but she grabbed his hips. "Brann, does it hurt? Be honest."

She gripped him with her hand again and he groaned, unable to answer her with words, so he simply shook his head. She hovered over him and sheathed herself with one movement, bringing herself up and down, up and down, her slick juices torturing him until he nearly climaxed, but he held on.

"Ye first, my sweet," he said through a clenched jaw.

She rode him hard, taking him deeper with each thrust until he finally reached between them and teased her in just the right spot, forcing her over the edge with a moan. He bucked against her as his own orgasm coursed through him, and he buried himself deeper, giving a hoarse shout as he took his pleasure.

When she was finally able to move, he helped her off of him, and she reached between them and pulled the condom off, holding it away from her. "Now that wasn't so bad, was it?"

"Hellfire, the dick cover worked."

CHAPTER THIRTEEN

WHEN ALLIE WOKE UP, SHE couldn't stop a moan of pleasure from leaving her mouth, memories of Brann's lovemaking last night possessing her.

The man had a tongue to die for, and she'd learned something new about herself.

She was indeed multi-orgasmic, since she'd had the rare pleasure of three orgasms within an hour. The man was also an insatiable beast.

She reached for him, surprised when her hand didn't find him. They'd gone to sleep spooning, but they'd both floundered in the huge bed until he'd wrapped an arm and leg around her, almost as if he were afraid she'd leave him.

Which was exactly what she'd told him she planned on doing. She'd shared her revised plan to leave today, and he'd reminded her of her promise to stay longer. She'd insisted.

And yet…he wasn't in the chamber, and she missed him already. How would she feel when she returned to her own time?

She climbed out of bed, doing her best to straighten her wild waves with her fingers

When was the last time she'd used a comb? Jinty hadn't given her one, so she assumed there weren't any. There was still some water in the pitcher at her bedside, so she poured some into a bowl and washed her face. She then swished her mouth with water, using a linen square to rub her teeth. When she finished, she ate the few random limp mint leaves Jinty had left on the chest, hoping to improve her breath. How she wished for some mouthwash.

She snorted.

Or a toilet or a shower or a sink or a tooth-brush…the list was endless. Not wanting to search through the chest to find appropriate clothing, she put her bra on and wrapped Brann's plaid around her waist, throwing the end over her shoulder. She stepped into the passageway and heard a gasp. Jinty. The maid was running toward the stairs, a pile of linens in her hands.

"Cover up, lass," she said over her shoulder.

"Where's Brann?" she shouted at Jinty, hoping she'd answer.

"Outside heaving with everyone else," she yelled back.

Oh, that couldn't be good. Just the thought of someone heaving made her hurry back into her room. She used a big squirt of hand sanitizer and found a bland blouse in the chest to wear with the tartan. Once she felt properly attired, she grabbed Smoky and headed down the stairs.

"Come along, wee one, though it's not all about you this morning. I'll have to check on Brann and the others. You recall my nursing career, don't you?" Smoky stared up at her and gave a soft bark as if to agree with her.

Why was everyone heaving?

She hurried down the staircase, Smoky tucked in the crook of her arm. The hall was nearly empty, which felt like a bad sign, and two lasses were scrubbing the floor in a few spots. She headed straight out the back door, almost banging into Elspeth.

"Oh, Elspeth. Do you know where Brann is?"

"He's out back heaving, and 'tis about to rain. I hope it pours buckets to wash all of the sick away."

"Have you been sick at all? Or any of the other maids?"

Elspeth stopped, folding her hands in front of her. "Nay, I have no' been taken with it. One of the lasses is ill, but no' as bad as the lads. They are all heaving, some in the front, others in the back."

The back of the keep was a mess of grasses, weeds, and bushes, with various paths leading through it, but she managed to find him in the far corner by the curtain wall. She passed a few others lying on the ground asleep. She hated to ask what had been going on while she slept part of the day away. Brann lay flat on his back, his arm covering his eyes against the light of day. "Brann?"

She sat down cross-legged, settling Smoky between her legs.

"Brann?" she whispered, reaching over to place her hand on his forehead. His skin was damp but not overly warm. "Are you all right?"

His arm moved and he peeked out of one eye, groaning slightly. "Ye arenae sick?"

She gave it a passing thought and said, "Well, I'd have to say my belly is a bit queasy, but I'm not sick."

A sudden noise alerted her to another person vomiting not far from them, the sound forcing Brann to roll onto his belly. "Nay, no' agin."

He emptied his stomach. In between heaves, he muttered, "Ye need no' stay, lass. I can die on me own."

Smoky stared up at him each time he started a fresh round of heaving.

"How many others?" she asked.

He wiped his mouth with his sleeve, spat into the grass, and said, "I've got to get an ale."

"No!"

"What?" He stared up at her, his eyes rimmed with dark circles, his skin ashen.

"No ale. That could be what caused your sickness."

She helped him to his feet, scooped the puppy up, and followed him to the keep, glancing around to see how the other men fared.

The sky turned gray and big fat drops of rain plopped onto the broad leaves on the tree Brann had paused to lean on. He waved his hand toward the door. "Go. Get ahead of the rain. I'll be along in a moment."

Food poisoning of some sort must have done this. The only way so many people would get sick simultaneously was if they'd ingested the same thing around the same time. It had to be something from dinner. The problem made Allie's mind feel like it would explode. It would be difficult to determine the cause in a world with no refrigerators. But she knew where to start—the kitchens.

She opened the door, surprised to see Cook hard

at work in the back. Cook handed her a bowl of porridge, steaming and full, and she shifted Smoky beneath her arm so she could take it. "Oh, thank you. Cook, you aren't sick?"

"Nay, but nearly all the guards are. I'd stay away so ye dinnae catch the heaving from them. I told them they had to keep out."

Her mind rushed through everything she knew of microbiology, but she could only think of one way to address the problem.

"Cook, would you boil the water the guards will be drinking today? Make sure there's a huge pot of boiled water for them to drink."

"Boiled water? Who wishes to burn their mouths on boiled water? Are ye daft, lass?"

"No, you don't understand." Sometimes, it frustrated her too much to try communicating in the medieval form of Scots, but it was important for her to focus today. She had to make sure they comprehended her instructions. She'd teach them a few things about hygiene, including the importance of washing hands and boiling water. On the other hand, maybe she'd just tell them what to do and not try to explain why. Other than Brann, no one would ever believe her story about microbes.

"Clearly no'. I'll no' be killing our men." Cook shook her head, her indignation obvious.

"No. You need to boil the water for at least five minutes. Then you can cool some for drinking, while the rest can be used for cooking. It's the only way to get the heaving to stop. We don't know what has caused this outbreak, but we need to get everyone hydrated, and the safest way would be for them to drink water that's had all the germs killed."

The door opened and Brann stood there, looking exhausted.

Cook glanced at him. "Chief, ye look awful, but yer woman is talking nonsense. I dinnae know of what she speaks."

Brann looked from Cook to Allie. "What's so confusing?"

"I asked her to boil the water before everyone drinks it. It's hard to explain, but it's safer. So many of you are sick and you need fluids. You're less likely to get sick from it if it's been boiled first then cooled."

"Ye want Cook to boil just water? When 'tis fresh from the well or the streams?"

"Yes. You all need to drink water, and we can't risk it being inf…dirty. Getting you sicker. Please?"

Brann began to turn green and quickly said to Cook, "Just do as she asks. Please." He ran out the door without a backward glance.

She tried one more time. "Please, Cook? It's really important. If you'd like, I'll boil it. But so many of the men are sick."

Cook shook her head and motioned her out the door. "Take care of our chief. I'll do as ye ask."

She glanced at the bowl of porridge in her hand, wondering if she should risk eating it. "Cook? Did Brann have porridge?"

"Nay. He was heaving before he had the chance to eat. 'Tis why I have so much still in the pot. Nae one is eating."

She sighed as she filled a bowl of milk for Smoky. Good, the porridge should be safe, and it was one of the most palatable foods in medieval times. She made her way back into the empty great hall.

Sighing, she set the porridge down and squeezed Smoky. "Besides, porridge has been cooked. It should be safe."

Then she held the little dog's face up close to hers. "What do I do? Stay or go?"

She knew in her heart she'd never be able to leave so many sick individuals. Her trip home would have to be postponed a few days.

Two days later, Brann strode into the hall and made haste to the table where Allison sat, followed by Angus and Hamish, one of his best guards. They needed to strategize after all that had transpired.

One of the few guards who'd found his way in to break his fast was talking to her, a bowl of porridge in his hand. "Are ye sure I'll no' start heaving agin, my lady?"

"When was the last time you heaved?" Her pet dog sat in her lap and she stroked the little dog's coat.

Reminding him of how well she had stroked him the other night.

Forcing his thoughts back to the present, he shifted his gaze from her fetching eyes.

"Last eve. I slept the night through and me bowels…"

Allison held her hand up to stop him. "That's all I needed to know. If the porridge is hot, you'll be fine. Just eat it slow and stay away from the ale. Water only until tomorrow is what I would recommend. Your chief will find another cask of ale by then."

Brann glanced at the other men in the hall. They'd all had quite a nasty bout of sickness, so he understood their hesitancy to eat. Many men had not even come to break their fast. "Allison, will ye join us in the solar? I have some questions for ye."

She stood, settling Smoky in her crate, and cooed until the dog was nearly asleep. Why did the lass insist on torturing him? He ran his hand down his face and spun on his heel, heading toward the door.

He'd wait for her outside the solar. He'd forced himself to stay away from her because he didn't wish to give her his sickness. No matter that she'd insisted he and the others were ill because they'd eaten something she hadn't—he still didn't wish to risk it. She'd promised to stay until they were all hale, so he knew he'd tempt her into one more interlude before she left.

Or so he hoped. If not, he'd be chasing her to the faerie pool.

She stopped in front of him before she entered. "Are your insides finally improving?"

"Aye," he said, not wishing to remind himself of all his suffering. He ushered her inside and moved behind the desk. His men stood on either side of him, and Allison took the chair across from his desk. "Are ye still confident 'twas the cask of ale?" he asked her.

"Yes. It seems the most likely culprit based on my interviews of all your clanmates. Was it tightly sealed before it was opened? That could have caused it to turn."

"I opened it and 'twas no different than any other, Chief," Angus said. "But mayhap 'twas a bit loose. Honestly, my mind is sickened and I cannae recall."

He stared at the floor, obviously embarrassed over his failings.

Hamish added, "Every man who was sickened had the ale, and the sickest drank a few goblets. We've been drinking the boiled water as my lady has suggested. The men have come to trust what she says."

Brann hated to hear confirmation that the cask was the culprit. He knew it to be possible as making ale required quite a bit of care. This was a gift he'd received from Murray, who had been his friend these many years. Could the Sinclair have been right after all? Had the ale been tainted apurpose? Rubbing his hands together before he spoke, he mulled over his options.

"Angus, when ye can, find ten guards who are hale and patrol the area. I know no' who is our enemy at present, but we must be prepared for an attack from anyone. I dinnae like to have so many of our men unable to fight."

"Are ye nae going to attack them for this?" Hamish asked, clearly offended by the affront they'd all suffered.

"Nay, no' yet. I will visit the Murray on the morrow and put this to him directly. Ye know the MacKays and the Murrays have always been strong allies. I'll no' believe Ewan Murray did it intentionally unless I hear him admit it with my own ears."

"Poisoned ale is no' reason enough?"

"Poisoned ale is reason enough, but do we know he did it intentionally? Until we know, we'll no' act on it." Brann stood. "Go on yer way, and find men to help protect what's ours, Angus. Find men that can assist ye this day, though I know 'twill be difficult. Leave Hamish behind to handle the remaining men. We're limited today because some did no' heed my warning and continued to drink the ale. I'd like to speak with Allison alone."

His men nodded and left the solar.

As soon as they were alone, he peppered her with questions. "If I take ye to Murray land, can ye tell if he's the guilty party? Can ye tell if Murray did it alone or if one of his men did it? Can ye search his keep and find the truth?"

"No, I'm sorry, Brann. I can't even test the ale—I'm just basing this on observation and questions posed to the victims. But I definitely think it's a good idea to travel to Murray land. It would be worth it to see if they are sick as well."

"Understood." He took a deep breath before he voiced the matter that weighed most heavily on his mind, despite the possibility of an impending war. "Can I convince ye to stay until Lachie returns? He'll be upset if he finds ye've left without bidding him farewell." What he thought but did not say was that he'd be upset, too. "We lost more than two days to sickness."

Her gaze caught his and hope flared inside him, hot and bright. Hellfire, she was one beautiful woman. He had to convince her to stay. "We have one con…one of those things left." He waggled his eyebrows at her.

"Are you asking me to stay to help with the poisoning or because you want me in your bed again?" She tipped her head to the side.

"Both?" Needing to be closer to her, he circled around his desk and then tugged her out of her chair. With Allison cradled in his arms, he sat on the desk and held her close. They stayed like that for a while, tucked into each other, and then he tipped her chin up and kissed her, a soft kiss meant to tell her she was more than just a woman in his bed. Not a man accustomed to speaking his feelings, he couldn't find the words to explain how she'd caused an ache inside him he was unable to quash—how the damn thing bloomed to something larger every time she was near. He canted his head to the side instead, devouring her as though she were the sweetest of nectars.

He was not ready to lose her yet.

He ended the kiss rather abruptly because he feared it would lead to more. When she stumbled and fell limply against him, he couldn't help but puff his chest out a bit. Had he convinced her to stay? "Just a wee bit longer? Please? I'm hoping that convinced ye that I wish for ye to stay for many reasons."

She cuddled into his chest, tucking her head under his chin. "One more day. But I wish to travel with you to Murray land. Promise me you'll take me, or I'll return to the pool today."

"Why would ye wish to go to Murray land if ye cannae determine the Murray's guilt? 'Tis no' safe for a lass to be out away from her clan."

She pushed away from him to gaze into his eyes. "Because there's an off chance my sisters might be here, too. The more I think about it, the more sense it makes. I thought originally that I was the only one who fell through the portal. But after what you told me about your parents, I've considered other possibilities. What if they landed somewhere else and made it to a neighboring clan just as I did? One of my sisters could be living on Murray land and another on Sinclair land. If I go, I would recognize them. Maybe it's a long shot, but I'd never forgive myself if I went home only to find out they were still here."

"I'll take ye along, but ye must promise to stay near me or Angus. I'll no' have some bastard stealing ye to be their bride."

"Agreed. I don't wish to marry anyone either."

"Aye, so we'll go on the morrow," he said, stepping away from the desk. His face broke into a wide grin. "But what can we do now? I think I need to be checked out by my healer."

"Who's your healer?" she asked, following him because he hadn't released her hand yet.

He spun around to look at her. "Ye are my healer, lass, and I need to have ye check my body." He led her up the stairs and toward his chamber, but stopped to whisper in her ear, "But no' before I make ye scream my name three times."

She pushed at his chest lightly. "You know, I didn't care before because I was in a hurry to return, but what will your men, your serving lasses, even Jinty think of me? They must hear me in your chamber. It wouldn't be so taboo in my time, but surely it is here. They must think I'm a whore."

He tugged her back against him and said, "My people will do as I tell them, but I'm willing to concede to yer sensibilities."

"Good. We'll wait until this eve after everyone is sleeping." She melded her body against his just the way he liked.

He chuckled. "Nay, I'll smother yer screams. 'Tis

my only concession, lass. Ye know ye want me as much as I want ye." He whispered the words in her ear and she whimpered as she rubbed against him.

"Lass, ye have nae willpower." He kissed her cheek, because he quite liked her that way.

She sighed, a sound that came from her toes. "I know."

"Please never change."

CHAPTER FOURTEEN

ALLIE SIGHED AS SHE SNUGGLED against Brann's chest, playing with the dark hair there. The man was something else in bed. "Do you know that in my time, lots of men shave their chest hair?"

"Why in blazes would they want to do that?"

She shrugged. "It's just become the way of it. Men have to work out lifting weights to bulk up the way you are." She traced a finger across his huge bicep. "They don't spend their days lifting heavy swords, so they have to do it another way. Some of the younger women don't like the hair so much. They even shave their own hair."

"The women have chest hair?" he bellowed.

"Nay, not chest hair." She pointed to the pubic region. "There."

"Why the hell would they wish to do that? That would make them look like bairns."

She shrugged her shoulders again, enjoying his honesty about her modern culture. "Makes some things easier."

He shook his head and climbed out of her bed.

"I dinnae think it should be too difficult for a man. Dinnae shave yers. 'Tis short enough."

She decided to drop the subject. He peeked out the small window, completely bare-assed but without an ounce of shame. Then he spun around to stare at her. "Now I'm curious. Will ye show me what else is in the bag that had the dick covers inside?"

She couldn't help but giggle at his term for a condom. Dick Cover. She should trademark it if she ever got back.

She rolled out of bed and reached for the bag still sitting on the chest. Plopping it on the bed, she opened the bag and dropped the contents into the middle of the coverlet she'd rearranged.

"May I see the bag?" he asked as he sat down next to her. She handed it over, and he felt it between his fingers, his brow wrinkled in confusion. "What is this made of? 'Tis quite strange."

"Plastic. Nothing natural, but if you close that seal, it should be watertight." She showed him the workings of the zipper-like mechanism. He opened and closed it three times before he finally set it down.

"That alone convinces me ye are from another time. We have naught like that here. What are yer other valuables? I dinnae see any gold coins." He touched the various items, waiting for her explanation.

"Our money is paper."

"What's paper?"

She said, "Never mind. Just know that it's more portable than gold coins. You can fold it and hide it."

"So what is inside these containers?" He held up the pill container, shaking it lightly.

She held her hand sanitizer. "This cleans your hands if you don't have soap and water available."

"But I thought ye said water was piped every-where."

"It is, but still, you could be in a car…" She glanced up at him, realizing too late that she'd only made things more confusing.

"A car?"

"We still have horses, but a car goes way faster. It's a bunch of metal sitting on top of four wheels. You can drive a car wherever you wish to go, but there's no water inside."

"Ye mean like a cart?"

"Yes! Exactly like a cart. But it's covered so you can travel in the rain without getting wet."

"But yer horses will get wet."

"No horses. It's motorized." She stared at him. "Never mind. Let's move on. So the condoms are gone, unfortunately, but I have some things for sicknesses."

"Why did ye no' give it to me? Would it have cured me of the heaves?"

"No. These are specific." She held up the naproxen. "This is for inflammation, and this one—" she held up the amoxicillin, "—is for an infection."

"What's that?"

"As I tried to explain when you all got sick, there are millions of tiny creatures living around us that we can't see. Different kinds. Some can be harm-ful, others are helpful. This will kill the really bad ones."

"So why didn't ye give it to us?" He held one pill

bottle up and shook it. "These little things would kill millions of creatures?"

"Yes. Those kill bacteria. But it won't help cure everything."

He held up the glass vial. "And this?"

"An antibiotic. I would put this directly into your vein. It's very strong."

"How do ye remove the top?"

"You don't. I would need a syringe, a type of needle, to get it out, but they broke on the trip."

"What are these wee things?"

"Bandages. Small portable ones that will stick to your skin." She held up one of the bandages so he could look at in the light. "They have an adhesive on the back to make them stick to your skin. It keeps the dirt from getting into a wound. It would be beneficial for you in the lists. If a man has a cut, it might keep it from turning bad. You've seen wounds that get all full of pus? White stuff and green stuff?"

He nodded.

"Well, these could prevent that from happening."

"Why did ye bring all these things to ward off sickness? Are ye that worried about getting sick?"

That statement made her realize something a bit frightening. "I'm not worried about me. I brought them for my sisters in case they needed help."

"So ye would no' use these things if ye needed them?"

Dammit, she was just one giant caregiver, wasn't she? To her patients, to her dad and his diabetes, and now to her sisters. "No, I'd save these things for them."

"They're more important than ye?"

She scowled, not knowing how to answer his question. Fortunately, he didn't wait for her answer.

"Nae more dick covers?"

"No. You know what that means…"

His expression turned serious. "Tell me ye won't go yet. Stay a little longer."

She turned her head away. "I'll go to some neighboring clans with you to look for Caroline and Hannah, but if I don't hear of any new lasses nearby, I'd like to go back."

"I'll plan a trip to Murray land for the morrow, but ye should wait for the next festival before ye go."

"Festival?"

"Aye, we have a festival in a sennight. The one where the women are allowed. 'Twould be yer best opportunity to look for yer sisters. All the neighboring clans will be there."

"All right. I'll stay, but just to look for my sisters."

He arched a brow at her. "But no dick covers… what will we do?"

She scowled, only because she knew that would be difficult for her.

"There are other ways, as ye know, lass. I need not plant my seed in ye to make ye yell my name." He whispered the last part so close to her ear that she shivered, but she pulled away, not wanting to hop back into bed with him just yet.

She pasted a smile on her face and said, "Of course there are." However, she had no willpower around him. She knew what he did to her. She'd be begging him in no time.

No time at all. She would not get pregnant in the fourteenth century.

He brushed her arm and kissed her cheek. "I'm going to the hall so I dinnae do what I shouldnae at the moment."

As soon as he left, her gut clenched. It wasn't his quick departure that upset her, but the revelation he'd brought out of her—she cared more for her sisters than she did for herself. Something was wrong with that.

Why didn't she like herself?

The next morning, Brann led a group toward Murray land. He'd given everyone strict instructions on how they were to conduct themselves, especially Allison. He still feared some fool would try to steal her away and marry her, which was part of the reason he'd insisted she ride in front of him.

The other reason he didn't like to admit. He liked being close to her.

He noticed her gaze searched far and wide as they rode, probably hoping to see one of her sisters. He didn't blame her. He'd do the same if he were in her shoes.

He'd comb the island from one coastline to the other if Lachie ever went missing. Even Taran's disappearance would affect him more than he cared to admit. This he decided to ignore.

Taran was dead to him.

They drew closer to the gates, and Brann waved his hand to indicate the horses needed to slow down. Something wasn't right. Murray guards always greeted anyone who approached their land.

No one had greeted them today.

He had a sick feeling in his gut as he approached the gate, which only worsened when one warrior, pale in color, came out to greet him.

"I'm here to visit yer chieftain."

The warrior leaned on the curtain wall, clutching the stones as if to prevent a fall. "Go home, MacKay. We're all sick. If ye come in, ye'll be sick, too."

Brann motioned for his men to turn around. He couldn't put his men through the same sickness or a different one either. "We'll return in two days."

Allison didn't agree with his decision. "Wait, Brann. If it's the same sickness you had, we can't catch it."

Angus said, "I'll stay out here."

Brann arched his brow at her.

"Fine. Help me down and I'll go see by myself."

"Nay, I dinnae want ye going inside," Brann said. "Ye'll risk getting us all sick."

Allison said, "Brann, I can't explain it all to you, but just trust me. I need to see if I can help at all."

"Nay." He was not about to risk her safety. She'd just have to follow his orders.

She twisted around to stare at him. "I know you like to be bossy," she whispered, "but not about this. I'm going inside to see if I can help. I've been doing this in some form or another for several years. I won't risk exposing your clan to another round of sickness, but I'm getting down and you aren't going to stop me."

Before he could argue, she slid down the side of his horse so quickly she almost fell over when her feet hit the ground. Her abrupt dismount neither stopped nor slowed her, and she took off in a run toward the guard at the gate. "Open up. I'm here to help."

"How can ye help us?" the guard atop the wall asked.

"Have you just opened a new cask of ale from the same batch you brought to the MacKays?"

"Aye, we celebrated a betrothal at high sun the day before. And we need to drink ale today because we've been heaving so."

"Then I can help. Let me in." When he didn't jump to do her bidding, her hands went to her hips. "You think because I'm a lass I cannot help? Or are you just a fool? What person in their right mind would refuse help?"

The guard glanced over at Brann to get his approval, a shocked expression on his face.

"Ye'll no' allow this, will ye?" Angus asked, his horse prancing a wee bit from his master's agitation. "She could get us all sick again."

Brann glanced up at the guard and nodded. "Open the gates. I'll go with her."

"Ye cannae risk yerself! Ye're the chief," Angus said.

"Angus, can ye no' see he has the same sickness we had? Murray brought us the cask. The ale sickened his men just as it did ours."

"But mayhap they *did* poison us apurpose."

"Why would they poison themselves, too? I think this proves Murray's innocence. Something else happened to those casks, and we need to discover what. Take the rest of the men home. I'll stay inside the gates with Lady Allison. When she gets a notion in her head, it doesnae leave her."

Angus studied him for a moment and then nodded "I'll leave a few men a ways out to escort ye back."

"Aye. We shall return before nightfall."

The gate opened and Allison rushed inside without waiting for him, headed straight for the hall.

Angus said, "I dinnae know where she came from, but the lass has bigger bollocks than most men."

"Aye, she does," Brann murmured, watching her march across the courtyard with purpose and determination.

"Ye'll have yer hands full if ye convince her to stay. Ye ken that, aye?" Angus said, a knowing gleam in his eye.

"I do," he said, staring after her.

"If ye need anything, send a few men back to me, and we'll have more men here as fast as we can." Angus turned his horse around and motioned for their men to follow him.

Brann led his horse into the stables and settled him inside with some oats since there was no one around. What the hell was he to do with Allison?

Stubborn, sassy, strong-minded, intelligent, passionate—these were words he would use to describe her. If anyone had asked him what he wished for in a mate, the only one of those words he would have thought of was passionate.

Before they'd met, he had thought of only one thing—being recognized as the strongest warrior in all the Highlands. That hadn't changed, but it had been a lonely life, fighting at the corners for all to see, traveling to long-distance fairs to fight. Despite what Shona had done to him, he wished for companionship, for a true partner.

Strong men needed strong partners. A strong lass like Allison would surely give him strong sons, something else he yearned for but didn't like to admit, especially after the mess with Shona. How many times had he heard of weak women dying in childbirth, unable to bear the pain and succumbing for whatever reason?

Not Allison. Allison would roar that child out of her, and it would be a strong bairn with a husky cry. There'd be no need for a wet nurse to take over for her. She'd be strong enough to feed three bairns, if he had to guess.

For the first time in his life, he pictured himself with a woman at his side and many bairns surrounding them—and he liked what he saw.

He shook his head to jar the thoughts from his mind. Relations with the lass had weakened him for certain. He climbed the stairs and entered the great hall—an empty great hall. Murray's kitchens were attached to the hall, and he could already hear Allison's strong voice barking orders to the Murray cook about boiling water.

He moved inside the kitchens, surprised to find only two workers inside. As if the cook read his mind, she glanced at him, totally confused.

He stood behind Allison and set his hands on her shoulders. "We had the same illness at my keep. The people who got sick all drank from a cask of ale given to us by yer chief. Allison had us all drinking water after it had been boiled, and we improved within a day. I'd listen to her."

Allison glanced at the two Murray servants, one and then the other. "Did you drink any ale?"

Both women shook their heads. "We dinnae, but

the men did. Most of them."

"Don't drink it and don't allow anyone else to drink it. Have you any bones left? Venison or mutton? I think it would be best to start some broth cooking. Maybe only put in a few carrots. Keep it bland."

"Where's yer chief?" Brann asked.

"In his chamber. He hasnae moved since last eve."

Brann said, "Boil a large pot of water for ten minutes, then let it cool. 'Tis all yer people should have today. Mayhap they'll be fit enough to drink the broth by this eve."

"Only if they've stopped heaving," Allison clarified. "Once they've stopped for half a day, they can try the broth."

"Aye. We're going to visit with yer chief."

Before they left, Allison spun around and said, "And only cooked porridge and broth on the morrow. They must eat slow. And more water. No ale for two days and open a new cask."

They found Ewan Murray lying on his bed, his eyes in a vacant stare.

"Ewan?" Brann asked.

Allison moved over to the bed and set the back of her hand on his forehead.

"I'm dying."

She pulled a stool over next to him and sat down, holding his hand in hers. "No, you're not dying. You're sick from the ale in your cask. Either it wasn't sealed properly or you made some mistake in the brewing process, but I promise you that if you don't drink any more ale, you'll survive. Your men, too."

It was a testament to the man's illness that he

looked not at all surprised by Allison's accent nor her brash, direct manner.

Brann said, "We went through the same at our keep. We opened the cask ye brought over and drank it that night. Dozens of my clanmates were sick the next day. We narrowed it down to the ale. Everyone who had taken sick had drunk a goblet of ale. Ye did, did ye no'?"

"Aye. Two goblets. My men have been coming back inside for more, Cook said. Please tell her to stop it. Have someone empty it into the dirt." His skin was pale and drawn, his eyes dull.

"Allison has already given Cook her instructions. She's boiling water to drink and cooking broth. Yer men should have naught but water and broth and porridge for a day or two."

"Then we'll live?" The tremor in his voice reached out to both of them. Brann couldn't believe his friend's weakened state. How fortunate for his own clan that they'd had Allison at their side.

Allison's voice took on an even more commanding tone. "Look at me."

Ewan turned toward her voice.

"How much ale have you had?"

"Two goblets before I started heaving, then I had another in the middle of the night. I swear I have naught left to heave."

"If you don't have any more, then I promise you that you'll survive. Don't drink any more ale, just water, and when you haven't heaved in half a day, try some broth. I promise you'll get better if you don't drink any more ale."

Ewan's gaze stuck on hers, and Brann thought

he could detect a slight misting in the chieftain's eyes. "My thanks to ye. Will ye tell my men no' to drink the ale?"

"Yes. We've told Cook already, and Brann will tell the men we see on the way out."

"Are ye sure I willnae die? If I do, I wish for Brann to take over my land, split it with Taran. I have nae sons. I have not yet married."

Allison patted his hand. "Nonsense. You need not think like that."

Brann continued to watch the woman in front of him, awed by her. Her tone of voice was magical, the calm force Ewan's soul needed in the midst of the chaos. The soothing words, her small ministrations—they all did their work in a way he'd not seen before.

Allison was definitely something special.

On their way out, they spoke with the cook again, along with several of Murray's men.

Brann paused before they were ready to leave, then turned back to Cook. "Have ye seen any new lasses here recently? Have any women joined yer clan over the last two moons, Cook?"

"Nay," she said, "I would recall a new lass."

Only one question persisted that he couldn't answer.

Who had set out to poison both the Murrays and the MacKays?

CHAPTER FIFTEEN

ALLIE'S MIND TORTURED HER, JUMPING
from one thought to another. She'd admitted
to Brann that she would save the necessary medicine she'd brought for her sisters, which essentially
meant she valued their lives more than her own.

But another thought made her feel quite ill.

She'd almost left Clan Murray without giving a
thought to her sisters. Hadn't that been the reason
she'd agreed to stay with Brann? She'd planned to
spend the next few days asking around about them.

Only she'd forgotten.

She hadn't given her sisters another thought
because she'd been so wrapped up in helping Clan
Murray.

Had it not been for Brann's question to Cook,
she'd have no idea whether or not one of her sisters could be there.

Guilt riddled her nearly senseless. Why? Why had
she forgotten something so important?

"Stop torturing yerself," Brann said, his horse
moving at a nice canter through the valley.

"What? What makes you think I'm torturing myself?"

"Because I can feel it in ye, lass. When ye get to know someone well, ye know how their thoughts turn before they do sometimes. Ye were worried about a clan of sick people thinking they were all dying. And I commend ye for taking the time to calm their laird's fears."

"Thank ye…I mean, thank you." Dammit, now she was talking like them. If she assimilated any more, she may as well stay.

"Ye were a healer in yer time, aye?"

"Sort of. The nursing profession developed for many reasons, but we have doctors and nurses and a few levels between them. The doctors assess patients and decide how to best treat them. Nurses fill a very different role. We administer some of the doctor's orders, but we also help the patients deal with their situation, teach them how to adapt their lives to a sickness, and offer comfort where it is needed."

"Ye have wonderful comforting skills."

"That was my favorite part of nursing. Anyone can give medicines. Tell me more about the festival next week."

"There will be many people there from the four bordering clans, but also visitors from beyond. Merchants and vendors attend to sell food and wares. 'Tis a way to build yer coffers if ye have skills to market, or if ye can compete well."

"Compete? What kind of competitions? Please tell me you aren't going to fistfight ten men." She turned around to give him a glare. "Blows to the head can do permanent damage, you know." He'd told her about his barbaric competitions.

"I'll be competing in other areas. No fistfights. 'Tis too much for women's tender sensibilities. We do archery, the log toss, and an obstacle course for horses and their riders. There will be sword fights, but 'twill be to first blood only, not to the death."

"Who sets up all the contests?"

"People who want more coin. There will be plenty of wagering. Ye must pay to enter, and others wager on who they think is best. The winner and second best will usually get a part of the wagers."

"And you think my sisters would attend such an event? It doesn't sound like it would be appealing for most women."

"Och, but after they win their wagers, they take the lassies to the vendors' booths and buy them sweet treats or ribbons for their hair. I've seen woolen garments sold, even fragrant oils or candles. There will be much to see, and 'tis where ye should spend time looking for yer sisters."

She couldn't wait to go.

Brann led the group to the festival, though Angus rode on one side of him and another warrior rode on the other. Hamish had stayed home to protect the keep. They still hadn't discovered how the casks had been tainted, but he wouldn't give up looking. In fact, if he had the chance to speak with Sinclair at the festival, he'd be sure to tell him all alliances were off. He'd make no promises to anyone until the culprit was found.

In truth, he'd much rather spend time with Allison than play this game of alliances. Much to his frustration, she'd insisted on sleeping in her own bed once Lachie returned. They'd only shared one brief lovemaking session since then, and there had been no seed-planting involved. Allison did not wish to carry a bairn.

It had left them both wanting more. If she were staying, he'd ask her to be his wife. Then he'd plant his seed freely and thoroughly. He smiled at the thought of having the strong woman as his wife.

Wishing wouldn't make it come true. But if they could find one sister, perhaps he could convince her to stay.

One sister. He had to begin his search in earnest.

Lachie had been returned home on time, much to Brann's relief, and he now rode alongside him, babbling the way he often did. He could tell his ramblings delighted Allison, though he couldn't explain exactly how he knew that. Sometimes he felt he knew everything about the lass, and other times, he felt he knew nothing.

"My lady," Lachie said. "I'm glad ye made Smoky fat enough that her mother accepted her. I could see how happy she was to feed with her brothers and sisters. But I told Jinty she has to make sure Smoky's doing well while we're gone."

"I'm sure Jinty will keep an eye on her." She tipped her head back to the soft breeze flowing across the meadow. "The air just smells better here."

"What?" Brann asked. "How could that be?"

She glanced at him with a smirk on her face. "I don't know how it's possible, but it smells better here."

"I'm glad I came home so I can travel with ye,

Brann," Lachie said. "I'll be by yer side when ye compete. Which contests will ye enter? Probably most of them. Mayhap ye shouldnae enter them all so someone else can win some prizes. Ye know ye are the best in the Highlands at everything, but ye should let someone else win. Are ye going to enter them all, Brann?" He paused for a brief second, and when he didn't get an answer right away, he added, "Well, are ye?"

Brann chuckled. "If ye take a breath, I'll answer ye, lad."

Lachie frowned for a moment before perking back up again. "Go ahead. I'll wait for yer answer."

"Careful, Lachie, or ye'll fall off yer horse. I'll enter the log toss, and mayhap the sword competition. I'll leave the archery for others. Will that suit ye?"

"But what about the horse race, the one with the obstacles? Star is the best at that. I told Taran he'd lose to ye."

That meant his brother would be attending, along with Shona, and he'd have to listen to people's laughter and taunting. Worse, he'd see the pity in their eyes.

Allison gave him a sidelong glance, but he ignored it. He knew she wanted him to forgive his brother.

"If Taran is racing, then mayhap I will, too."

"Are ye going to be nice to our brother? Please, Brann? 'Twould mean so much to both of us. Shona feels badly about what happened."

Brann ran his hand down his face. "Lachie, 'tis enough for now. Ye are making my head ache." A thought popped into his mind and he was surprised he hadn't thought of it before. "Lachie, was there any sickness at Taran's when ye were there?"

"Nay, just me."

Allison's head pivoted faster than his own. "What sickness? You weren't drinking ale, were you?"

"Nay, I had the red throat."

"The red throat?" she repeated, unable to mask the little bit of concern in her voice.

Brann felt his brow furrow. Why would she be upset if he was better? Did she know something they did not?

"Aye, just for three days, but I'm much better now."

"Did you have a fever? Headache? Anything else?" she persisted.

"I did have a fever. Taran said I burned his hand." He chuckled as he spoke. "My throat hurt really bad and my head hurt, but I'm better."

Allison said, "I'm glad you're feeling better. Let us know if you feel worse at the festival." Her words were comforting, but Brann was tuned in to her body language, which signaled the opposite of her words. She was worried for some reason.

"Was anyone else sick, Lachie? 'Tis verra important," Brann said.

"Nay, just me. I dinnae go near Shona. She stayed in her chamber when I was sick."

"You knew enough to do that?" Allison asked.

"Aye, 'twas what Brann and Taran always said. Stay away from others when ye're sick." He turned his head and a broad smile crossed his face. "Look at all the tents. This will be the biggest festival ever! They're waiting for Black Brann, I'm sure of it. Ye'll show them in the log toss and the sword skills. I'll sign ye up as soon as we arrive. Ye'll take care of my horse?" he asked, turning to Angus.

"Go, laddie," he said with a nod. "I'll take care of yer horse."

As soon as they were close enough, Lachie jumped down from his horse, tossed the reins to Angus, and took off toward the center of the festival.

The closer they came, the louder the chants grew. "Black Brann, Black Brann, Black Brann!"

It occurred to him then that he'd made a mistake. He'd been so eager for her to stay that he'd overlooked a crucial problem, something he'd never cared much about before today.

This festival was infamous for bride stealing.

Allie couldn't contain her surprise at the size of the festival and the massive throngs of people drifting about the grounds. On the far hill, she could see tents and colorful banners all the way to the top. On another field, merchants had set up tables and tents to market their wares, their loud voices carrying across the crowd. She couldn't contain her excitement either. "If my sisters are anywhere in the area, they'd come here for sure. They'd be looking for me the way I'm looking for them."

He found a cool spot under some trees for their horses and motioned for his guards to take care of them. "Allison, what will ye do when ye find them?" As he spoke, he guided her away from his men.

She'd been hurrying down the empty path, but his words caused her to stop and face him. "Brann, you know I've wanted to get back to them from the beginning…"

"Aye, true. I know ye'll go back through the portal if ye dinnae find them, but what if ye find them here? What if they've found shelter with another clan? Will ye leave me to join them?"

She stared at him, her mouth opening and closing before she whispered, "Honestly, I don't know. I…we…do you have feelings for me? Would you want me to stay? But I'm sure they'll want to go back. Hot showers, cell phones, airplanes. They're probably looking for me with the same intention. Once they find me, we'll all go back."

"What if one has married?"

"Married? My sisters? They wouldn't marry so quickly."

Or would they? Caroline wouldn't, but what about Hannah? What if she found the right man here in medieval times? Would she want to stay?

And if Allie could be here with at least one of her sisters, would she want to stay, too?

"Brann, I don't know how to answer your question. If we don't find them, I won't need to answer, so let's wait and see."

He placed his hand at the small of her back and ushered her ahead of him toward the festival grounds. Once they made it to the vendor booths, the crowd thickened. Allie moved ahead of him, eager to look for her sisters, but Brann didn't let her get very far. He stayed right behind her, and at one point he even tugged her back against him. She swatted him, but he continued to trail her. His attitude was positively…medieval. A couple of men had taken notice of her, but their attention was nowhere near as disturbing as Sinclair's had been.

Then, out of nowhere, he shouted, "She's mine!"

Several heads snapped around, none faster than hers. "What did you say?"

"Allison," he growled. "Ye haven't noticed the attention ye're getting. I've warned ye about bride stealing in these parts. Any unattached lass is considered fair game for a marriage at these festivals. I'm just attaching ye to me. Unless ye wish to find yerself in someone else's marriage bed at dark, I suggest ye allow it."

She opened her mouth to argue, but it finally registered that he was right. The men near her appeared to be salivating at the sight of her, their grins enough to tell her exactly what they were thinking. True, she didn't wish to be controlled; after the issue behind Brann's castle, she decided to change her viewpoint.

She turned back to the fools and said, "Did you not hear him? I'm his."

She glanced over her shoulder, noticing he was doing his best to stifle his smirk, pleased at her announcement yet still doing his best to keep his angry disposition for the men around him. He had a reputation to uphold, that of Black Brann, so he quickly restored his mean face.

Men.

He escorted her to a food vendor and bought several tarts. When he offered her a berry one, she nearly grabbed it. "Blueberries?" she asked with excitement.

"How the hell would I know if they were blue?"

She stifled a laugh as she bit into the tart—and

then immediately moaned, unable to stop her reaction to the sweet concoction. It was easily the best thing she'd eaten in the fourteenth century.

He yanked her over to stand in front of him with her back to him. "Ye cannot continue to do that or ye'll embarrass me."

She noticed his erection right away and managed to wiggle her backside against him, giving him a saucy look over her shoulder.

He squeezed her hip to hold her in place. "Not funny, lass."

She straightened her back and finished her sweet tart while he ate a plump meat pie. "These are not blueberries, by the way, but whatever kind they are, they're heavenly."

Lachie came tearing up to them and said, "Brann, I signed ye up for the log toss and the sword contest. The log toss is first. Oh, and the obstacle course for the horses. 'Tis after the log toss but before the sword fights. The log toss begins in fifteen minutes."

"We'll be right there, Lachie. Do ye wish for a tart?"

"Aye," he said, grabbing one and running off. "My thanks, Brann," he hollered over his shoulder.

"Aren't they called cabers?" she asked, remembering something she'd read in a guidebook about Scotland.

"Aye, in Gaelic, 'tis a *cabar*."

"And doesn't it have to be a special kind of tree?" she asked, a bit of berry juice trailing down her chin.

"Nay, they're logs. Fallen trees…any kind…" His gaze followed the juice, and she could tell he was seconds away from lapping it up. Had they not been in such a public place, she wouldn't have objected. She used her finger to swipe it off instead, then allowed him to grab her hand and tug her along behind him.

Medieval men. One needed to be careful around them. She swore Brann had the testosterone level of ten men of her time.

"I'd love to watch you," she admitted. Though she was grateful he couldn't wrestle with anyone at the festival, she did look forward to watching him display his prowess and skills.

"Good. Now can ye promise me ye'll not look at any other men while I'm competing? If ye do, I'll be distracted."

"I promise. I'll not draw any attention to myself."

She couldn't have been more wrong.

CHAPTER SIXTEEN

ALLIE KNEW SHE COULD KEEP her promise because she would be busy looking for her sisters. Brann led her over to a spot where Lachie would stand, and he gave Angus instructions to stay by her side. The vantage point was ideal for searching the crowd, so she didn't really care.

However, her attention was diverted as soon as the next competitor was announced.

Black Brann MacKay stripped his tunic off and moved up to take his spot against a huge burly man who'd just won the last round.

And just like that, Allie couldn't shift her gaze off him. Brann's torso was covered in a light sheen of sweat which highlighted his every muscle, every curve and valley. She'd done her best to taste much of him over the past week, but she'd clearly missed some areas. He swaggered into the small arena, flexing his muscles and working the crowd as he moved, using his best fierce glare to intimidate his opponent. The crowd chanted his name, but she barely heard it, too intent on the grace of the testosterone-loaded specimen of maleness prowling in front of her.

For God's sake, she could barely control herself around the man. He launched his first log into the air, clearly beating his opponents. There were four men in the first round, and one was eliminated after each toss. The crowd worked itself into a frenzy as Brann won round after round.

Allie finally tore her gaze from him, shifting her attention to the sea of excited faces gathered around the arena. There were no familiar faces.

Nonetheless, she would not give up.

The crowd continued to push inward as more and more men and women were drawn to the contest by the shouts and roars of festivalgoers caught in the fever of Black Brann. She saw a flash of hair that put her in mind of Caroline, so she pushed her way to the side of the crowd, leaving Angus and Lachie. As she got closer, though, she realized she was wrong. She stood there for a moment, feeling on the verge of tears, and out of nowhere, an arm snaked around her, tugging her backward.

She raked her nails across the hand at her waist, kicking one leg back at the brute, trying to connect wherever she could, but without much success. The other men in the crowd ignored her, which was nearly as frightening as the initial attack.

Were they oblivious to the fact that she was being attacked, or did this happen frequently enough in medieval times that they simply didn't care?

Even though the contest was still underway, Brann heard her scream and drew his sword with a growl, heading straight for her. Miraculously, the arm released her and the crowd parted to make way for Brann. She hurried toward him, throwing herself at his chest.

As he wrapped his arms around her, she distantly heard the head of the contest declare Black Brann the winner since there were no other contenders.

The horde of onlookers fell back, heading toward the main thoroughfare of merchants and vendors. Allie clung to Brann, not wanting to move. She preferred to stay in the one place where she felt safe and loved.

Dammit. What the hell should that tell her about her feelings for Brann?

She expected a tirade to erupt from his lips any moment, but it didn't happen. He rubbed her back as she nestled in beneath his chin, not wanting to step away from him for a moment. "I'm sorry, Brann I thought I saw someone who looked like Caroline, but it wasn't her. I don't know how I ended up so far from Angus."

"I know. 'Tis no' yer fault, lass. 'Tis the fault of the bastard who grabbed ye. I'd like to find him. Do ye think ye'd recognize him again?"

She stepped back to look into the eyes of this man whom she trusted more than anyone. "No, I never saw his face. He grabbed me from behind. The only thing that could give him away is that I scratched his hand and his arm. How many more things have you to do?"

Out of the crowd, a man came forward. From his tentative manner and his big green eyes, she knew this must be Taran. She'd seen him outside Brann's castle, but not up close. Those were Brann's eyes.

"Brann, I saw the altercation. Is she hale?"

Brann's entire body tensed at the sight of his

younger brother. "Allison, meet the man who used to be my brother, Taran."

"My lady." He nodded to her but then shook his head sadly. "Ye need to let this go. I could have been protecting her."

"I'll protect her myself. I dinnae need yer help. Did ye see the man who tried to steal her away?"

"No' well, but he wasnae that tall. Brown hair, which is the same as most of the men here."

"Taran, I'll not be participating in the sword contest. I'll not put her at risk again. Ye'll probably win it easily."

"And the obstacle course?" Taran quirked his brow at Brann.

Allie could see this comment upset Brann. "Go ahead," she urged. "I'll be fine. I promise not to move from Angus's side this time."

Brann seemed to consider her comment, then nodded to Taran. "I'll compete in the horseman-ship contest. I'll have all my guards surround her, stay with her. I'd allowed some of them the chance to get food." He turned his attention back to Allison. "Do ye agree to stay inside my guards?"

She nodded quickly. After the last debacle, she wouldn't leave Angus's side.

Wrong again.

Brann's jaw clenched the moment he spied Shona, Taran's wife, coming up behind them with three of her husband's guards.

"Greetings to ye, my lord."

Brann nodded to her, unable to speak. He

squeezed Allison's hand and tugged her closer. But the sight of her didn't beleaguer him as it usually did. The pain he felt was mostly remorse for having lost his brother. When he realized he was free of much of his anger, he said, "This is Allison. She and her kin were attacked by reivers, and most of them killed."

Taran frowned. "My sympathies, my lady. 'Tis most difficult to bear the loss of a family member. I understand exactly how ye must feel." He gave his brother a pointed look, but Brann ignored him.

Allison just nodded, her gaze alighting on Shona.

He could almost feel the jealousy emanating from Allison's pores, but she had no reason to envy her. Shona meant nothing to him. Had his brother not gone behind his back to court her, he might have even been relieved she'd chosen Taran.

But his own brother had betrayed him.

"Taran, I'll see ye on the obstacle field." He ushered Allison away, a voice carrying from behind him. Lachie had returned. "Brann, may I go to the fields with Taran?"

"Go with him," he called over his shoulder. "'Tis fine, Lachie."

He led Allison over to the vendor tents, keeping his arm around her waist. "See anyone who looks familiar, lass?"

"No. Would you lead me to the end of the vendor tents, please? The one at the end looks busy, and I can't see everyone in the crowd. The colorful blue one. Do you know what tent that is?"

"Aye, 'tis the rock toss. If ye land the rock square on a piece of wood, ye get the prize."

"Oh, I love carnival games!" she said, her word

choice puzzling him. "What are the prizes?"

"Different things. Usually ribbons or meat pies or ye can have the seer tell ye what's to come for ye later in life."

"Like a fortune-teller? A psychic?"

"A what? I dinnae know about that, but we have seers. Some are talented, some are false. Ye take yer chance. They take yer coin and tell ye what ye wish to hear is my guess."

"Oh, I want to try and win a reading."

He shot her a look, his familiar ye-cannae-do-that look. Sure enough, he said, "Ye cannae do that."

"Why not?"

"Because 'tis for men only. We win and give our prize to the lass. Shall I try to win ye some ribbons for yer hair?" His crooked grin made her laugh, even though she hated that she couldn't play herself.

"Fine, you can win for me if we must do it that way." Her scowl amused him. He'd wager she probably could win on her own, though he didn't know many other lasses capable of such a feat.

They arrived at the booth, probably the largest one there. The woman running the booth was gray-haired and wide in the hips, though she had eyes that looked as if they could see right through to your soul. There was something else odd in her gaze, though he couldn't quite decide what it was. On one side of her booth she had a multitude of ribbons, and turkey legs and apple tarts were arranged on the other.

"Win something for yer lass?" She waved Brann right over.

Allison asked, "If he wins, will you tell me my future?"

"Future? Nay, I'll not tell ye anything. If ye win, ye get turkey legs, ribbons, or apple tarts.

Brann said, "I'll try. I'll take the turkey leg if she doesnae want it."

Allison's heart sunk, but she shrugged and stood back to watch him as the crowd cheered him on. Brann managed to land his first rock perfectly. While she applauded him, a warm breath whispered in her ear. "He's searching for ye."

She spun around, expecting to see the old woman there, but she stood a good distance away from her, an odd smirk on her face. "What did you say?"

The old woman held both hands up. "I dinnae say anything."

But Allison knew better.

Brann won two more rounds before they told him he could win no more. He turned around with a huge smile on his face, wrapping his arm around her. "Ribbons or turkey legs? We have three coming."

Rather than answer, Allison leaned close to the woman running the booth. Up close, she thought the woman's eyes were a different color, but she stepped away from her quickly. "Are you a seer?"

Brann froze next to her, waiting to see what the woman would say. She shook her head. "My apologies, but the seer did not come with us today. Choose something else."

Allison nodded and selected her two ribbons

while Brann chomped happily on his turkey leg. As the woman handed the ribbons to her, she said, "There are much better ones in Edinburgh. I'm sure ye'd find exactly what ye're looking for there."

Allison was so befuddled she didn't know how to respond. Having completely missed the subtext of their exchange, Brann wrapped his arm around her waist and moved her down the path toward the armorer's tent.

But not before the woman gave her one last piece of advice. "Ye should go to Edinburgh. He'll find ye if ye do not."

Once they were far enough away not to be heard, she turned to Brann. "I swear she whispered something in my ear when you were tossing your rocks. She said a man is searching for me. Who could it be?"

"Did ye ask her?"

"I did, but she claimed she'd never spoken to me. Oh, Brann. I'm so confused, but thank you for my ribbons. I need them." She couldn't help but glance back at the strange woman one more time. Was she a seer or not?

Allie shuddered. She'd already been grabbed twice.

Who was after her?

They hadn't gone far when Wallas Sinclair caught up with them, the fury in his gaze visible from across the field. He ushered them away from the eavesdropping crowd into an empty clearing off to the side, not far from the obstacle course.

"Sinclair," Brann said. "Ye are troubled about something?"

"Aye, I am,"Wallas said."Are ye a traitor, MacKay? I see ye chatting with the enemy, yer brother."

"A traitor? Ye dare to call me a traitor?" Brann thought his head would explode, but not before he choked Wallas Sinclair so he could watch him draw his last breath. He had to let go of Allison's hand because his fist had clenched so tight it had to hurt. She stepped back but stayed close.

"Aye, ye are allied with me, not yer brother, and I just saw ye speak with him."

"He's my brother," he sneered, his face now a hand's length away from Sinclair's. "And I'll talk to both of my brothers as I please. If ye cannae accept it, then abolish our alliance." He wasn't honoring the alliance anyway, but if he could get Sinclair to reveal his intentions before they settled this, he'd be a wise man.

"I'll accept it if ye swear ye arenae planning agin me."

"Yer name was never mentioned. We spoke of the contests. But I'm glad ye are here. Are ye the one sending men after my lass?"

"What? Why would I send someone after yer lass? I offered for her and ye rejected me. I accept that from my ally."

"Because a man grabbed me behind the keep the day you were there,"Allison said with a haughty air about her. "Did you send him?"

Brann jerked his head around at this new piece of information she'd just revealed. Fear of what could have happened was quickly followed by anger. She hadn't mentioned a thing.

"What?" Brann asked. "Ye were attacked on my land and ye dinnae tell me?"

"Ye allow her to speak?"

He spun around to face Sinclair and said through clenched teeth, "Aye, I allow her to speak. I trust her words more than I do yers."

"Now ye call me a liar?"

Before he could respond—or lose his temper and punch the bastard—Taran came up beside him, followed by Ewan Murray.

"Do ye need help, brother?"

He couldn't believe it. Taran had come out of nowhere acting as though they'd healed their differences and would carry on as they'd always done, just in time to give credence to Sinclair's accusation. He hadn't intended to honor his commitment to Sinclair, but he hadn't had the time to travel to Sinclair land to speak with the man. This wasn't how he'd wanted to end the alliance, but after hearing Allison's revelation, he didn't care.

"Nay, I can handle myself and I dinnae need help from any of ye. And aye, she's my lass, and aye, she can speak if she wishes." He spun on his heel to face her. "Now, who attacked ye on my land and what did he do? I'll flail him until he has nae skin, here in front of all. Just name him or point him out. Was he wearing the Sinclair's plaid?"

She stared at the plaid the chieftain wore. "No."

"Aye, because he wasn't one of my men," Sinclair snapped, appearing even more infuriated than before.

"Brann, I did not see his face. He grabbed me from behind, but I fought him, kicked him in his bollocks…"

"Allison, do ye no' understand that when I declare ye as mine, the declaration carries with it the promise of protection? That I'll let nae one touch what's mine?" Stepping away from the others, he drew his sword so he could swing it over his head and connect with the ground, releasing his anger. What else could he do?

Murray stepped in and said, "We're all here for a festival. We need no' kill each other. After all, Brann's clan and mine have just healed from the sickness. He brought his lass to help my men heal."

"Ye are in with the Murray, too? And what sickness did ye all have?"

"I'm nae in with anyone!" he bellowed. "All alliances are off, no matter who ye are."

"What has ye so upset, Brann?" Murray asked.

Allison reached for his sword arm, rubbing it up and down in an attempt to calm him. It wasn't working.

He'd kill the man who'd dared to touch her.

Twice.

CHAPTER SEVENTEEN

DESPITE THE STICKY WEB OF alliances and lies he'd found himself in, only one thing mattered to Brann. He fought to calm himself before he turned around to Allison, took her hand in his, and said, "Tell me. I need to know all about this man or men who have attempted to abduct ye. I dinnae care about the rest." Looking up at the others, he said, "Ye can all fight it out. It doesnae matter to me. *She* matters."

She blinked and he could see the misting in her eyes that she fought to hold back.

"I'm sorry I didn't tell you about the first attack. I was too focused on…well…everything else. As soon as I stepped out your back door to go to the kitchens, he came up from behind me, grabbing my waist. Just as this one did. I fought them both off."

Brann whispered, "Was it anyone ye recognized from our clan?"

"No, he ran away over the curtain wall. If it was the same man, why would he wait until now to try again? There would have been other opportunities, especially when everyone was sick."

Brann resheathed his sword and rubbed his hand across his brow. He wrapped his other arm around her and turned to the three men still standing nearby. "I want ye to find out who did this. It had to be one of yer clanmates. Nearly every man here is a MacKay, Murray, or Sinclair."

"Or MacDonnell," Sinclair said.

Brann had forgotten about Shona's clan. Perhaps someone felt he hadn't honored his agreement with their clan chief because he'd allowed her to go to Taran.

A whistle near the obstacle course beckoned all of the contestants to come forward.

Brann said, "All alliances are off until I find out who did this to Allison. I want to know."

Taran and Ewan headed off to get their horses, but Sinclair held back. As soon as he was sure they were out of hearing distance, he said, "Ye'll regret this. I'd planned on using our alliance after this festival."

"Until I find out who's attacking Allison, everything is off."

Sinclair gave him a long look, no doubt trying to intimidate him, and then nodded and headed off toward the last race.

She reached for his hand. "I'm sorry, Brann. I should have told you, but I really did forget."

"Think on it. Mayhap I'll not ride in this competition."

At that moment, Lachie tore over, waving his hands urgently.

"Go ahead," she insisted, squeezing his hand.

"I promise not to move from Angus's side. Make Lachie happy."

He kissed her forehead, and they strolled over to the obstacle course together, hand in hand. Lachie threw his arms around them, then took up Allison's free hand, swinging it. They found Angus, and Brann gave him the instructions for his guards—they were not to leave Allison alone for even a moment. Before he left to fetch Star, he scanned the crowd for a long moment, looking for anyone who appeared out of place.

No one stood out.

He took care of Star, pampering him like a bairn, praising him, rubbing him down, and feeding him an apple, which he took with one bite. Then Lachie snuck him another one. There were ten challengers. The two with the quickest time through the obstacle course would go head-to-head at the end, and the champion would be declared in front of the crowd at the end of the festival. This win would give Brann two wins, and he'd probably be declared the festival champion since the other two contests had been won by two different men.

He made it through the first round with the second-best time. But to his dismay, Taran had come in with the best time.

He would go head-to-head against his brother. That forced him to pace.

"A ten-minute rest and the finals will commence," the announcer declared. Taran made his way toward him, but he intentionally turned away, grabbing Allison by the hand and heading over to the drinking well.

"Brann, I really wish you'd mend this disagreement between the two of you," she said. A little line formed between her brows, something that oft happened when she was vexed with him. "I understand why you were upset at first, but you should be over it by now. If nothing else, it's in your best interest to have your neighbor as an ally, not an enemy."

He swallowed a long drink and spat most of it out. "I dinnae trust any water unless 'tis boiled. Someone taught me that." He gave her a lazy grin and pinched her backside.

"Yikes," she squealed in reaction, taken aback by his pinch, though it hadn't hurt a bit. "You pinch?"

"Nay, I just like to touch, and it has been a while since I've been able to touch ye the way I like. My hand lost control so close to yer skin." He waggled his brows at her, a sly grin on his face. "Believe me, there are many other things I'd rather do to ye."

She narrowed her gaze at him, crossing her arms in front of her chest as if trying to decide exactly what she wished to do with him. "My, but you are a horny beast."

"A what? Yer sayings. I just dinnae understand them."

"Horny. Someone who wants sex all the time."

"Aye, then. Call me horny if ye like," he whispered, giving her another teasing rub along her sweet bottom. "But only for ye." He nibbled on her earlobe, and she sighed in that gusty way he loved.

"You are distracting me on purpose."

"Is it working?"

The gleam in her eyes told him she liked to tease. "Aye…nay," she said. "Dammit, now I'm talking like you. Could you please make up with your brother? You need to get over this."

"Nay. Could ye please stop cursing?"

Ignoring his attempt to take her off topic again, she took a step back and put her hands on her hips. "Why won't you repair the relationship with your brother? You know how much it would mean to Lachie."

"Because he betrayed me. Brothers dinnae betray each other."

"Or is there another reason?"

"What other reason could there be?"

"Are you jealous? Because if Shona is the true reason, then you should demand that she return to you. Then you'll have a good reason for being furious with one another. But this, this is just someone trying to make his brother suffer."

"Ye think I want Shona?" Could she be telling the truth? He'd seen that wee bit of jealousy in her eyes earlier. "Shona and I couldnae be more different. Nay, I have nae interest in her."

He saw the brief look of relief flash across her features before she spoke. "Then end this thing. Please, for everyone's sake. You know how I miss my sisters, and it hurts me to see you and your brother at odds."

He paused, then reached over to run his fingers through her hair. "I'll consider it, but no' until after the race. Will that satisfy ye for now?"

"For now, I suppose. But I won't let up. And neither will Lachie. You've put him in a most difficult position."

The whistle sounded, so he kissed her and said, "I promise to consider it later."

He hurried back, leaving her with Angus and his men.

Brann was so damn stubborn. How could she have fallen in love with a man who was this stubborn?

Her eyes widened and her insides did a full flip. Who the hell had suggested she loved him? She moved closer to Angus as she watched the two men get ready for the final race. A bit uncomfortable in the big crowd, she frequently glanced behind her just to be certain the MacKay guards still surrounded her.

Her gaze returned to the man now on horseback in front of her, sitting astride his beast with confidence. He had a way of melting her heart from a distance, enough so that her eyes teared up at the thought that he cared for her.

Somehow, she'd done something right in this strange land, something she'd been unable to do at home. She'd managed to attract a proud Highlander, one who wasn't afraid to speak his mind, one who was brave and honorable yet knew how to be tender and gentle, one who was all man but treated her as his equal.

He was perfect, and as crazy as it sounded, she *did* love him. She wasn't ready to tell him, but even saying it to herself made her break into a wide smile. He'd accept his brother eventually—he was too softhearted not to, though she'd never tell him so.

Lachie danced from one foot back to the other

while he waited for the race to begin, his gaze ping-ponging from one brother to the other. A moment later, the referee holding a sword between them lowered the weapon, and the two brothers took off down the obstacle course, leaping over fences and streams and cutting sharp corners. The sight of Brann on his horse was exhilarating—the man was like one with his beast, exhibiting a surprising grace.

Out of nowhere, another horse broke through the trees at the end of the field, galloping directly toward the crowd at the periphery. Then, at the very last minute, he turned his horse directly toward Allison. Shouts from the crowd blended together, becoming nothing but background noise, as her focus narrowed on the man who was now headed straight for her. A mask protected his identity, which couldn't mean anything good.

She tugged on the back of Angus's tunic as the other guards stood in a line in front of her as protection. But then the rider abruptly turned away. Her guards relaxed, but they did so too soon—the masked man spun back around, pushing his horse into the middle of the melee, and grabbed her. He tossed her across his horse and took off back toward the forest.

She screamed and did her best to sit up, digging her nails into the man's thighs through his trews, even biting and spitting at him, but he wouldn't let go. Once they were in the forest, he slowed a bit, but her belly was already aching from bouncing across the spine of the massive beast.

The sound of another horse came crashing through the forest behind them, loudly enough to startle her captor. She heard him utter one word, "Shit."

He grabbed her by the arm and lifted her off the horse, lowering her quite a bit before dropping her to the side.

She landed flat on her back, hard, and she couldn't breathe.

This was it. She was going to die.

CHAPTER EIGHTEEN

B RANN WAS ABOUT TO CROSS the line at
the end of the course ahead of his brother,
guaranteeing a win, when he heard a scream.

It was a scream he knew well.

A man had just lifted Allison up onto his horse.
She lay facedown across the beast's back as her
abductor galloped toward the forest.

Hellfire, he could lose her.

He glanced at the line in front of him. If he rode
for another minute or two, he'd win, but then she'd
be another minute or two ahead of him.

He turned his horse away from the course with a
growl, knowing he'd just lost to Taran, but it didn't
matter. He couldn't lose Allison. Not yet.

Not ever.

He rode his horse hard, pushing Star into a fran-
tic chase after the fool who'd kidnapped Allison.
Following the man into the woods, he set a fren-
zied pace, but just before he caught the man, the
bastard picked Allison up with one hand. He held
her in the air for a brief moment, lowered her

toward the ground, and then dropped her onto the ground and took off faster than a deer hearing the swish of an arrow.

Brann would kill the bastard for certain. He started to go after him, but one look at Allison, crumpled on the ground, stopped him.

She looked dead. Her eyes were closed, her chest wasn't moving. With regret, he glanced back at the perpetrator, taking in every last detail, and dropped to the ground next to Allison.

She still wasn't breathing.

"Allison!" He fell to his knees and shook her, now scared to death. What the hell had happened? Had she snapped her neck? Wounded her back?

Wild over the possibility that she could die in front of him, he gripped her shoulders, lifting her enough to shake her a wee bit. "Allison!"

Her eyes flew open and she grabbed at him, driving her nails into his skin. "Can't breathe…"

He finally let his breath out. "Ye must have had the wind knocked out of ye. Relax."

She shook her head, panic written all over her face, so he lifted her to a sitting position and set-tled her on his lap, cuddling her under his chin. "Ye'll be fine. If ye've never had it happen, 'tis most frightening, but 'twill come back."

He looked at her face, paler than he'd ever seen it, her expression full of trust that humbled him. "Ye scared the devil out of me. I'll kill that bastard when I catch him."

She finally gasped and leaned into him, her breathing beginning to return to normal. "He just grabbed me…He just…"

"Hush, lass. Ye've no need to talk. Ye can tell me

all about him later." Wrapping his arms around her, he acknowledged to himself that he never wanted to let her go.

Horses' hooves interrupted them, crashing into the forest. Angus came upon them first, Taran and Lachie fast behind him.

"What happened to her? Is she hale? Did ye kill the bastard?"

Brann glanced up at his second. "He threw her off his horse to keep me from catching him. I thought from a glance that she wasnae breathing, so I had to make a choice."

Lachie squealed, "He got away?"

"Aye, he's gone. I have nae idea who he is." He peered back at Allison. "Did ye recognize him?"

"No. I didn't get a good look at him. He wore a mask."

Brann stood up and helped her to his feet. "I'm taking ye home."

"May I stay, Brann?" Lachie asked. "I'll go home with Taran, be back in a few more days?"

Brann had never felt so defeated. "Do whatever ye must, Lachie. I'm keeping Allison at home until we find the villain who hurt her."

Later that night, Allie rolled over to face Brann. They'd slept in his favorite spooning position, and she'd fallen asleep for a short time, but now she was troubled.

What should she do about this huge hulk of a man who had stolen her heart? If she went back through the portal, she knew what would happen. She'd go home to her slightly boring job and predictable life, and she'd lie awake every night, remembering how it had felt to be loved by Brann MacKay.

Oh, he wouldn't say it, but what man did? She knew with every ounce of her being that the look he'd given her earlier, after finding her out of breath on the ground, had been the expression of someone in love.

Brann MacKay loved her, and if it was as much as she loved him, then she was one fortunate woman. She'd found the love of her life, only he didn't live in her world.

What could she do about that?

Her mind flashed to the woman near the merchant tents. She'd warned Allie someone was looking for her. Could she have been trying to warn her about the evil man who'd stolen her in the middle of the festival?

If so, perhaps she was a true seer. There might be something to her talk of Edinburgh. Even though the woman hadn't said a word about her sisters, Edinburgh was closer to Leannan Falls, so perhaps that's where she'd find more information about the legend—or maybe even a way to get back. Truth was she was in no hurry to return anymore.

She peered at the man who truly loved her for herself, trying to embed the memory of him in her mind, just in case something were to happen. Somehow, she knew this was it; this was her one chance for true love.

They hadn't fooled around because he'd been afraid he would hurt her because of the strain on her back from falling, and she'd fallen fast asleep.

But now, as she watched him in his sleep, she wished to beg him to make love to her.

She ran her finger across his bottom lip as lightly as she could, but the change in his breathing told her he'd awakened. Without opening his eyes, he whispered, "Did ye find another dick cover somewhere? Did ye have more hidden?"

"No," she said with a grin. That smile disappeared when she said, "But I don't care anymore. Make love to me, Brann."

His eyes opened wide, one brow quirked at her. "Truly? Ye arenae teasing me?"

"Not teasing," she said as she placed the palms of her hands together and rested them between her cheek and the pillow. "I love you, Brann MacKay."

His hand brushed up her arm, sending a cascade of shivers through her. "Ye make me question everything I've ever believed, lass. Is that what love is?"

"I'm not sure. It's probably different for me than for you."

"I'll make love to ye on one condition."

"What?"

"That this time, 'tis at my pace, and 'twill be mighty slow."

She rolled onto her back so she could stretch all the muscles in her body, her arms reaching overhead until they hit the wall. "I accept and look forward to your odd sense of torture."

Brann pulled himself up until he hovered over her, gazing into her eyes. "But ye will still beg me. I can promise ye that. Mayhap 'tis not torturous, but ye'll no' soon forget it."

"That sounds quite enticing, my lord." She ran the back of her fingers across the light stubble on his chin.

"Does it?" He settled his lips on her mouth, a slow, evocative kiss meant to let her know how much he enjoyed kissing her. His tongue darted out to find hers, and their tongues dueled until he could stand it no longer. He changed his pace to a deep, ravenous attack on her lips, wishing he could devour her and never let her go, anything to keep her here.

"Mayhap I'll tie ye to my bed and never let ye go," he whispered against her ear, and she shivered with a gasp. So pleased was he with her response that instead of kissing his way down her skin to her breasts, he used his breath to torment her, occasionally darting his tongue out for a quick taste of her.

Her hands found his shoulders and her nails dug into him with a bite, compelling him to take her breast fully in his mouth in response. He suckled her until she cried out with a throaty moan that went straight to his cock. If it were possible for the lass's passionate response to make him any harder, she'd just accomplished it with one sound.

His hand strayed down to the folds between her legs, finding her slick with need already. "Allison, ye are a horny beast yerself, are ye no'?"

"Yes," she whimpered, sliding her hands down to his biceps. "For you, Brann. You make me crazy with need. Take me now. I want you."

"Och, 'tis way too soon for that. Ye cannae beg

yet." His hand moved up to tease her nipples, his thumb teasing the taut peaks while his mouth trailed down to the vee between her legs. He teased her first with a flick of his tongue in the right place, then moved his hand down to part her folds and plunged his tongue inside her wetness, making her writhe with need.

"Brann, please. I want to come with you inside me. Please?"

"Ye will, I promise ye that."

"Please, Brann?"

"Ye're begging again. No' allowed." He returned to his task and suckled on her nub until she writhed so much, he couldn't keep her still.

He stopped and forced himself up onto his knees, trailing his hands back up her body with just the lightest of caresses, using more pressure in the right places. "Ye are so beautiful. Long legs, breasts that beg to be suckled. So responsive. Ye make me hard with yer throaty gasps."

"Now, Brann."

It wasn't a question, so he chuckled and settled himself over her, putting his weight on his elbows as he kissed her neck. Her hands gripped his backside, trying to tug him close enough, and she rubbed herself against him, her legs spreading wide until he entered her with one thrust.

"Oh," she said with a moan and a sigh of pleasure. "Again."

He did just that, pulling out, teasing her entrance, and then thrusting back in quickly and stopping. "Ye like this?" he asked, nuzzling her neck just beneath her ear.

"Oh yes," she murmured.

Brann had planned to torment her in such a way for quite a while, but his own need took over, forcing him to proceed a bit faster. He picked up his pace and rode her hard and deep, and she moved her legs to take him deeper until he thought he was in heaven.

"Lass, I swear I'll never get enough of ye."

Her response was a moan followed by her climax, her contractions bringing him to his own orgasm with a roar.

Barely able to balance his weight on his elbows, he fell against her, panting. He rolled onto his back, taking her with him, and said, "I swear if I die making love to ye, I'll die a verra happy man."

With her warm, curvy body wrapped tight in his embrace, her gasps from their lovemaking heating his skin, and the feel of his own heart pounding in his chest, he had only one thought.

He'd never be able to let her go.

CHAPTER NINETEEN

WHEN ALLIE LEANED BACK IN the tub in front of the hearth in her chamber, a long sigh rolled out of her mouth. Last night, Brann had made her squeal and moan like she'd died and gone to heaven—and then come back for more.

How she hated the turmoil raging through her body.

She missed her sisters, wanted a bath in a real tub instead of this cold metal monstrosity she sat in, but she also wished for love. Brann had shown her exactly what her life had been missing back in Maine. If she went back, she'd probably never find the same love again.

Maybe she could convince him to go with her. He'd love the showers, the cars, and he'd probably spend all his time at the horse races.

Who was she trying to kid? He would not fit in Mayport Bay at all. He'd be too big for her car, too loud for any shop, too gruff for…well…everyone but her. But he was her gruff, stubborn, braw, gentle Highlander, and she had no desire to leave him.

What was she to do?

A knock sounded at the door, and it flew open before she could respond. "Allison, we need ye."

She slunk down into the tub with a shriek until she realized it was only Brann. Still, she could see the outline of someone standing behind him.

"Brann? The door?"

He glanced over his shoulder—the outline revealing itself as Taran, his brother—then slammed it. "Ye need to get out." He tossed her a linen towel and grabbed another one to help dry her.

"What is it?" She stood there while Brann did a lousy job trying to dry her off, haphazardly wiping her down as he looked for her clothing at the same time.

"Lachie. He's sick, verra sick. Ye must fix him." Then his voice lowered to the barest of whispers. "I could not bear it if anything happened to the lad. He's all I've got. Ye must save him. Please."

This wasn't the time to argue with him about Lachie being the only one he had, but his choice of words did tell her that the boy's illness was mighty serious. She'd been right to worry about him at the festival. "Hand me the gown over the chair in the corner." She'd done her best to dry herself off before donning her shift and her panties. How she wished she had more pairs.

"Hurry. He's got these spots all over him." With that, he rushed over to the door and held it open for her, tapping his foot when she didn't immediately follow him. Taran must have gone off somewhere because the hallway was empty.

"Forget yer hair," Brann said, clearly irritated that she was trying to run her fingers through her wild waves. She grabbed a leather thong and tied it back out of her way.

"Let's go. Show me where he is." She followed him to a small chamber at the end of the passageway.

Taran and Jinty stood in the dark chamber, fretting over Lachie's bed. The shutters hadn't been opened, so Allie moved to the window and opened one, letting in the cool fresh air and sunlight.

Jinty, truly upset, hurried over to the window to close it again, dropping the fur over it. "Och, 'tis not good for the laddie. The air is bad, ye'll make him worsen."

Allie placed a hand on her shoulder. "No, Jinty. The air will not hurt him. I need the sunlight so I can assess him, and the fresh air could be helpful. It's a little dusty in here. Maybe you could clean a bit? Or how about some fresh water in the urn and some linen squares? That would be most helpful because he looks feverish."

The maid clucked her tongue and took off after the water. "Poor laddie."

Allie nodded to Taran. "He's been with you?"

"He sickened again this morn. I brought him to ye right away. Lachie says ye have special skills. I couldnae awaken him. He slept the night through and still wouldnae move."

Brann tipped his head toward Lachie, indicating he wanted her to see to her patient. She knew better than to explain the importance of finding out the history of the illness, so she made her way to the bed and sat down next to Lachie—something she'd never be allowed to do at her job.

"Lachie?" His eyes were closed, so she did a

quick assessment. Skin flushed but dry. A pinpoint rash at his neck. She suspected she'd find it on his trunk as well.

She took his pulse only to have Brann whisper over her shoulder. "There's naught wrong with his wrist."

She ignored him and continued her assessment. Breaths were shallow, only a little fast, and his heartbeat was also fast but regular. She stood and motioned to Brann. "Would you help me sit him up, please? I'd like to look at his torso. Tell me what he's had to eat since we last saw you, Taran. Has he been drinking any fluids?"

"He hasn't been hungry or thirsty. He wouldnae eat anything last night, and I couldnae awaken him for breakfast. 'Tis why he's here."

Jinty rushed back in with the urn. In a flurry of activity, she poured fresh water into a bowl on the chest and set a stack of linen squares down beside it.

"Jinty, would you bring Lachie some water to drink? But please be sure it's been freshly boiled this morning." The older woman nodded and left, pleased to have something to do.

Brann sat his youngest brother up and helped Allie remove his tunic. She found just what she'd expected. The rash covered the boy's torso, front and back, and both arms.

"Lachie?" she called.

He neither answered nor stirred. She laid him back down but didn't cover him because his body raged with fever. "Brann, could you dampen some linen squares and hand them to me, please?" While Brann grabbed the squares, she palpated the lymph nodes around his neck, not surprised to find some hard and swollen.

He did as she asked and she set the cool cloth on the boy's forehead before sweeping it over his cheeks and his neck and his chest. His eyes finally fluttered open. "Lachie, I want you to wake up for me. Just for a moment."

He opened his eyes at the same time Jinty returned with another pitcher and a goblet of water.

She held her hand out for the goblet. "It's not hot, is it?"

"Nay, I checked it. 'Tis cool."

Allie put her hand behind the boy's neck and sat him up enough to put the cool water on his dry lips. "Lachie, you need to drink this."

He sealed his lips shut and shook his head.

"Why not? You need liquid inside you."

He finally opened his mouth to speak. "Nay, 'tis too painful." His voice sounded strained.

"Does your throat hurt?"

"Aye."

"Is it as bad as the last time?"

He nodded.

"If you wish to get better, you'll have to drink the water. Drink for me."

"Must I?" The boy's eyes teared up and she was glad to see he had enough fluid to make tears. He was definitely dehydrated.

Brann came up behind her. "Aye, Lachie. Ye must drink. Ye'll be getting sicker if ye dinnae. Do as she says. All of it."

Taran, who stood on the other side of the bed, said, "Ye told me ye trusted her to make ye better.

Ye must listen to her."

Lachie drank a bit down, but his eyes misted all the while.

"Stick your tongue out for me, please?" she asked, peering inside, not surprised to see a white coating there.

"What's wrong with him?" Brann asked.

She looked at Taran. "You said he had red throat before?"

"Aye. But 'twas at least a sennight ago. He got better."

"He has it again. We call it strep throat where I come from, and it can cause serious damage to a person's insides."

"I've seen red throat kill people, yet others heal. Why?" Taran asked.

"It's hard to explain. Why don't you help Lachie drink and use the cool water on his forehead while I go to my chamber? I have something to help him feel better."

Taran took over, so she headed down the passageway back to her room, Brann right behind her. "Can ye fix him?"

"Yes," she said as she stepped into her room. "I can give him something to stop the fever, and I'll get rid of the red throat, too."

She opened the chest and pulled out her plastic bag of treasures. Spreading her items across the coverlet, she located the naproxen, taking one pill out with care, then found the amoxicillin pills.

"Ye're giving him those?" Brann looked at her strangely.

"Yes." She held up the single pill and snapped it in two. "This will stop the fever for half a day."

Lachie was big for an eight-year-old, closer to a ten-year-old in her time. She picked up the other bottle and opened the cap, pulling out a tablet and breaking it in half, but he stilled her hand.

"Ye said ye were saving those for yer sisters."

"I know, but Lachie needs them."

"Mayhap he'll not need those. Just give him the one ye have plenty of, the one that stops the fever. He may not need the other. Ye can still save yer pills."

"No. Strep throat could kill him. He already has what we call scarlet fever. Strep throat is caused by a nasty bacteria that will keep multiplying and attacking his body if it's not stopped. It starts at the throat, but then moves inward to the skin and the heart, even to the kidneys. I must stop it now. It's already causing serious damage to him, and he may not improve for a sennight. He needs a full round of this, at least seven days of medicine, or the bacteria could kill him."

"Lass, I dinnae know what to say. I respect what ye're doing, but I know how important it was for ye to save it for yer family. I thank ye from the bottom of my heart. Will it work for certain?"

"Yes. Let me give him this now so his fever will stop for several hours. The rest won't stop for a few days." She carefully replaced the bottles in the bag and placed it back inside the chest.

Returning to the small room at the end of the hall, she was surprised to find it empty except for Lachie, but he sat up in bed waiting for her, alert and aware. She sat down on the bed next to him, then filled his goblet and handed it to him. "I want you to take these tiny things. They're called pills, and they'll make you feel better in a bit. They'll get rid of the red throat, too."

She told him how to take the pill, but Taran came in before the boy could swallow them. To her surprise, he did a double take and said, "Where did ye get those things?"

She had no idea how to answer him, so she told the truth. "They're something I brought from my land."

Taran glanced at Brann, who'd just returned, and said, "Our mother had things like those."

She had no idea what to say to that. Brann had told her about their mother, of course, but this was the first sign that she might have come from modern times. It brought so many questions to mind that she didn't know which to ask first.

But this wasn't the time to ask.

Taran quickly said, "Ye are certain these will help Lachie, lass?"

She nodded, not willing to go into any detail at the moment.

"Since ye are certain, I'll head home." Taran said goodbye to his brothers and said, "I must get back to Shona. My thanks for helping my brother, Allison."

Brann said, "Taran, dinnae tell anyone of her special skills."

"Ye can be certain I willnae," Taran replied. "They'd think her a witch."

CHAPTER TWENTY

TWO DAYS LATER, BRANN WAS down in the great hall breaking his fast when Hamish flew in the door. "What is it, Hamish?"

"The Murray is on his way here with ten guards. Shall we allow him in?"

"Aye. When he arrives, I'll see him in my solar."

Brann grabbed his bowl of porridge and moved to his solar. He'd left Allison upstairs tending to Lachie so he could give some thought to other pressing issues. He had plenty to think about before the Murray arrived.

Lachie had improved enough that he'd actually asked for a meat pie last night. Allison had insisted he only have a simple broth with vegetables, and though he'd fussed at first, he'd eaten two bowls. He'd told her how much better his throat felt with the warm liquid on it.

The lad didn't know when to listen to someone. Just as Brann didn't know when to admit he loved someone. This had to be love. When he'd seen Allison lying on the ground and not breathing the other day, his heart had nearly stopped. He wanted her in his bed every night, by his side at every meal, and he just enjoyed talking with her. They'd sat in front of his hearth last night and chatted half the night away. And the way she'd so easily given up something she'd been saving for her sisters had astounded him. She was a warm and generous soul, without a doubt.

He'd even found himself thinking about having a bairn with her. She'd be a great mother, and give him strong sons, without a doubt.

What the hell was he going to do when she left him?

He'd have to convince her to stay with him, but he had no idea how to do it.

A few moments later, Ewan Murray burst into the solar. "We have trouble."

Brann couldn't help but frown. "Sit down and tell me all." Jinty appeared in the doorway, so he sent her off for some bread and cheese and ale.

"No ale for me," Ewan said with a shudder. "Boiled water only, please."

Brann couldn't help but grin at Ewan's declaration. He wasn't the only one clinging to Allison's advice.

As soon as he sat down, Brann pressed him. "What is it?"

"I heard that someone is planning to attack yer brother. There are two forces joining. They'll attack Taran first, then probably me, or mayhap ye."

"Sinclair or MacDonnell? Though I doubt Mac-Donnell would attack his own daughter's husband."

"I dinnae know. I'm guessing Sinclair is one of them. He was mighty upset at the festival when ye ended yer alliance with him. He must have found another to join him. But ye must help yer brother. He doesnae have many forces."

"Shite. Does Taran know?"

"I sent a missive to him. Ye have to do something. *We* have to do something."

"What can we do if we know no' who's attacking? People love to tell tales, so 'tis entirely possible that 'tis false."

"Are ye willing to go to his aid, the way ye should?"

Brann hopped out of his chair, feeling the sudden need to pace. He couldn't believe Sinclair would be this bold, this rash, just because he'd become angered at the festival. "My brother doesnae need me. He's too proud and as stubborn as I am. If I offer, he'll reject my help."

"Ye're dead wrong about that. I hope ye'll not lose your brother over this. Tell me ye'll support my clan if we're attacked. Ye have the most guards and the best fighters, and the sickness weakened our men. Will ye help me fight agin the Sinclair?"

"Aye, Ewan. Whoever 'tis, I vow to help ye in case of an attack. Now, I think 'tis best for ye to stay at home." He stood up and led Murray out of the room and then out of the keep. "But ye must promise to advise me if ye hear anything at all. When the attack is imminent, send a messenger to me."

When they reached the stables, Brann grasped the man's shoulder, doing his best to calm him because he was so unsettled. "I'll come to yer aid if ye need me. Ye only need to ask."

"Thank ye, Brann. I appreciate it." Looking him

in the eye, he added, "I hope ye'll do the same for Taran."

With a huge sigh, Ewan Murray left. He took Brann's peace of mind with him.

He had no idea what he would do if Taran was attacked.

Allison came out of the keep shortly after Ewan left. Should he tell her the truth?

"What is it? Something bad, I can tell," she said, dropping her voice.

Hellfire, could the woman read his mind?

"Not here. We'll speak inside." He set his hand on the small of her back and ushered her in front of him, doing his best not to arouse the suspicions of his clanmates, who were busy doing their daily chores—baking, weaving, caring for the horses.

Once inside the solar, he spun around and held her hands in his. "The Murray was just here. He's heard talk of two forces combining to attack our area, but he knows no' who the first target is."

"You?"

"They're unlikely to come after me first. More likely they'll attack Ewan or Taran. It must be Sinclair. Ye know as well as I do that he's greedy for more land. He was upset I cancelled our alliance, so he found someone else to join him. And Taran? I have no idea what condition his forces are in. I know he's been training them hard."

"Well, you have to help both of them."

He tipped his head to the side, lifting his chin. "Do I, now? And why is that, my queen?"

"Don't give me that shit, Brann. You have to help them."

"Cursing again, my queen?"

"Yes, because sometimes it's the only way you'll listen. You better help your brother if it comes to that." She stepped away from him and crossed her arms in front of her, a stubborn look on her face that nearly made him laugh.

"I vowed to help Ewan. Does that please ye?"

"Yes, that pleases me. But what about your own brother?"

He shrugged his shoulders, crossing his arms in front of him to mimic her pose. "I havenae decided about my brother. I doubt he needs my help."

"Either way, you have to offer it, if it comes to that. You're the eldest. It's up to you to mend the fences."

"'Mend the fences?' Where do ye get yer expressions from?" Brann would have to think about it. Before their falling-out, he would have leapt on his horse as soon as he heard the news. He could picture himself yelling at Angus to ready two hundred guards to follow him while he bounded up onto his horse and tore out of his gates.

He would have moved ten mountains and an army of warriors for him.

What would he do if it really happened now?

"Lass, my brother doesnae want my help any more than I wish to give it. I wouldnae be welcome there."

"That's bullshit."

He chuckled. "Bullshite? I've no' heard that said with such emphasis before. Ye're a lass of rare talents, Allison Sutton."

"Do not patronize me, Brann MacKay. You're trying to take me off topic. Promise me you'll go to him if he's attacked—and I mean to assist him."

He dropped his arms and spanned the small distance between them, tugging her arms down so he could hold her hands. "I cannae do that. I promise to help Ewan, but I cannae promise I'll help Taran."

Her eyes misted and she said, "Please don't force me to choose," tears now falling down her cheeks.

"Choose? What must ye choose?"

"Brann, I love my sisters. I'd do anything to be with them again. Your brother is here, and he needs your help. He wants to make amends. If you turn him away…I…I don't think I can love someone who values their family so little."

"So ye'll leave me if I don't help my brother? Is that what ye're saying?"

"Yes," she said, swiping at the tears still sliding down her face. "I'll go back. As much as I love you, that love will be ripped from my heart if you deny your brother."

"Ye dinnae mean that." He reached over and hugged her to him.

Her hands wrapped around his waist, but she still did not relent. "Yes, I do. Even though I'll want to stay, I'll return to the pool." Her tears turned to sobs, and she managed to say, "That I promise you."

He had to hope it would never come to that.

The next day, Allie brought Smoky for a short walk and then returned to the keep to visit with Lachie. "Smoky," she said, picking up the little dog, "what would I have done without you in this new world? I fear I may be leaving soon, but I'm uncertain. If I do, please don't be upset with me. Now that your mama accepts you, you have all your siblings to love, so you understand why I may have to return."

Smoky gave a yip as if to tell her she understood. How Allie wished she could ask for her sisters' advice about the stubborn man she'd come to love.

She walked through the keep in a daze, and when she reached Lachie's room, she made her way to the bed and plopped Smoky down next to him. "She's all finished, Lachie. Tell me how you're feeling."

"Better, but I still get so tired. I went to the kitchens for my porridge and could barely make it back up the stairs. My thanks for bringing Smoky. I think I'm ready for a wee nap, and I like it when she sleeps near me. She likes to cuddle."

"If you're tired, you should sleep. Your body is trying to heal itself, so you must do what it tells you to do. Another day or two and you'll be up and about as if it never happened. How's your rash?"

He lifted his tunic to peer at his belly. "I think 'tis better. 'Tis nae so bright and it doesnae bother me at all. Many thanks to ye, my lady Allison."

"You're welcome, Lachie." She ruffled his hair, but she stopped when she noticed a strange expression cross his face. "What is it?"

"I thank ye for other things, too. For saving Smoky. I dinnae like it when the mother leaves the runt to die. Ye saved her, and I think ye saved Brann as well." He dropped his gaze to stare at the puppy.

"Lachie, I haven't done anything for Brann. In fact, he saved me from the mob at the corners."

"Aye, ye have. Ye just dinnae know it. I wasnae liking my brother before ye came. Ye make him happy. He smiles when ye are around, just as he did before Taran and Shona married. 'Tis like having my brother back. I hope he never leaves." In the barest of whispers, he added, "I hope ye never leave us."

Allie got so choked up over his comment that all she could do was lean over and hug him. She couldn't tell the boy she'd never leave, because it might not be true…and she had this odd feeling that her heart was about to be ripped open, never to recover.

"You take a nice nap and I'll go check on your brother." She kissed his forehead, tucked him in, and left before the tears erupted.

Dammit, these people all tugged at her heart-strings. Why had she let herself get so attached to them?

She crept down the stairs, not wishing to attract attention, and made her way to the chair in front of the hearth. She sat there for a long time, staring at the flames warming the room, thinking about all the downsides to living in medieval times, but Brann kept popping up in her mind. Memories of their lovemaking washed over her, warming her from the inside out.

Unfortunately, she only felt more confused than she had before she sat down.

An hour later, shouts erupted from outside the keep, so she jumped out of her chair and ran toward the door, opening it to sheer chaos. Everyone was congregating outside the stables, so she rushed over to them.

Brann stood with Angus and Hamish, barking orders. She listened as best she could, though he slipped into Gaelic when he was upset. The stable lads ran in circles, saddling horses as the guards mounted and headed out.

Allie whispered to the man next to her. "Where are they going?"

"Clan Murray is under attack, and the chief is sending warriors to assist him."

"Who is attacking?"

"Sinclair and another clan. But there are men at Taran's, too."

"Are guards going to help Taran?"

The man looked shocked she'd asked. "Nay. He betrayed our laird. He willnae send men there. 'Tis Taran's problem."

Allie stood there transfixed. How could he?

She stepped back, moving away from the crowd, and surveyed all that took place around her. Brann, the man she loved, was the most magnificent leader she'd ever seen. Men ran around in confusion until he barked at them to follow orders. Once he raised his arms, the crowd instantly calmed, listening to his every word.

"Ye will go now under Hamish's instructions. Ye'll aid the Murrays against the invaders, whoever they are. I want ten women in the kitchens preparing food for warriors. This will no' be a small undertaking. Send yer husbands off with a kiss because they head into battle. This is a much larger task than I anticipated."

Numerous clan members hurried off to do as they were instructed, but others remained, waiting for him to finish. "Angus, ye will stay here with a force of two hundred to protect what is ours, but be prepared to send more if the attack is larger than expected. I also want a constant patrol on our lands."

Brann rattled off a slew of further instructions and men hurried to do his bidding, their chests puffing with pride to be among the most dangerous warriors in the Highlands.

And Brann? He stood there like a god, his dark hair curling around his collar, a slight sheen of sweat dotting his brow, as he made decisions on the fly without questioning himself. The muscles in his upper arms and his jaw flexed as he spoke, belying his calm demeanor.

She held her breath, waiting for him to say he would be going to his brother's aid. Despite what the man had told her, she believed in him. She thought he would do what was right. Instead, he strode over to her and said, "I'll ask that ye meet with Jinty and get yer supplies together. Yer expert healing will be needed later. Make sure we have enough food, enough boiled water, whatever ye need. I'll tell Jinty ye are in charge of making us ready."

Her heart dropped to her feet. He wasn't going to say a word about his brother. This man she adored was going to risk losing his brother—and her—forever because of his stupid pride.

"Your brother. Are you going to his assistance?"

His gaze caught hers and she wished to scream at him, pummel his chest, slap his head from the side, but she wouldn't do so in front of his men, his clanmates. "Lass, I told ye I wouldnae. I gave ye my reasons. Naught has changed since then."

She nodded, unable to speak. The biggest lump she'd ever felt had lodged in her throat.

If he would allow his brother to die, he was not the man she'd believed him to be.

One foot stepped mechanically in front of another as she forced her way into the stables. A stable lad tried to stop her, but she grabbed one of the horses that had been prepared for the men, then made her way to the mounting block and climbed atop the horse.

She tugged on the reins and the horse took her through the gates. She heard Brann yelling at her, but she ignored him, spurring the horse forward.

She was headed to the pool.

"I'm coming home, Hannah and Caroline."

CHAPTER TWENTY-ONE

BRANN WAS FURIOUS. HE MOUNTED his horse and shouted instructions before he went through the gate. "Angus, send a patrol of twenty men across our land. Ye're to stay here and protect the castle, but prepare another force of a hundred men to await further instructions from me and me only."

"Hamish took one hundred. That puts them all to use. Ye are headed after her?"

"Aye, so she'll no' get herself killed."

He headed toward the faerie pool, but even though he rode hard and fast, there was no sign of her. He traveled for what seemed like forever without seeing even a glimpse of another horse. How had she managed to get so far ahead of him? "Allison!"

She'd warned him, of course, but he'd hoped to call her bluff. A Highlander's pride was no small thing, and he couldn't simply lay it aside. Allison didn't understand that, but Taran would. He was quite sure his brother wouldn't want his help.

It didn't matter that Taran only had about a hundred guards while he had over three hundred.

Or that the guards who'd chosen to go with his brother had been the youngest.

Or that many had come from Clan MacDonnell, which meant they were not well trained.

Or that Taran had only been training them for a month.

A month…

Allison finally came into sight. He managed to gain on her a little, so he pushed all thoughts of his brother out of his mind, instead focusing on Allison.

They were closer than he'd thought. Before he knew it, they'd be there. If he didn't go any faster, he'd have to dive in and yank her out because he'd never allow her to leave him.

Never.

He loved her. True, he hadn't told her so, but she had to know how he felt. The night after the festival, he'd tried to show her how much he loved her, expecting to surprise her with his tenderness, but he was the one who'd been surprised.

He'd almost orgasmed just from watching her climax. When had that ever happened before?

Hellfire, but she'd cast a spell on him from the very beginning, enchanting him with strong feelings he didn't fully comprehend.

"Allison, stop!" He brought his horse up next to hers and she turned toward him, tears covering her cheeks. She shook her head and plunged forward.

He had no choice. Leaping from his horse, he dove toward her, knocking her to the ground with a thud. He rolled to try to take the blunt of the fall, pulling her on top of him, and they landed together. She didn't waste any time before getting up and running away toward the pool. It wasn't far away.

"Stop, will ye no'? Can we no' discuss this?"

Her shoulders shook with another sob, but she didn't turn around. "Allison, I love ye. Please dinnae do this." He had to convince her somehow. If she needed words, he'd give them to her. As long as she didn't ask him for the one thing he could not do.

The one thing he *would* not do.

She spun around and charged toward him, surprising him because she shoved him in the chest. Hard. "I just told ye I love ye and this is how ye react? Ye hit me?"

"I didn't hit you. I pushed you away."

"Why? Talk to me, please."

"Why? Because you're a stupid, stubborn man. You know what I want you to say. I'm happy you love me, but it won't matter if I have to go back, will it?"

"Stay. I dinnae want ye going back. Why, after all we shared, would ye walk away?"

"You don't understand, do you?" she asked, squeezing his arms and giving him a wee shake. "You didn't believe what I said about your brother, so you just dismissed it…dismissed me."

"Nay, I dinnae. Tell me."

"How can I love a man who won't make any effort to save his brother's life? Or haven't you considered that he might *die* today? Your brother could be killed, and all his men, and you're too proud to help him."

"He doesnae want me there."

"You think not? How would you feel in his position? Would you be so proud that you'd allow all your people to die rather than ask your own flesh and blood for help?"

"Nay, I wouldn't risk others' lives for my own foolishness." Hell, why did she bring up so many good points?

"Have you thought to ask him? No, your foolish pride is in your way. You're too worried that you'll look weak. You think the world expects you to never speak to him again because he betrayed you. No, we don't. Many of us expect you to forgive the poor man."

"He'd be offended if I did ask him. Yer reasoning is that of a lass, not of a warrior."

"So you do think he'd risk all of his clanmates' lives?"

"Nay, I dinnae, but it hasnae reached that level yet."

"You're not there, so you have no way of knowing. You must really trust Sinclair then."

All of a sudden, he had a sick feeling deep in his belly that she could be right. What if the bastard Sinclair had brought his men and two hundred more to kill all of Taran's people and take over his land? *MacKay* land. He'd told Sinclair he did not care what happened to his brother. He'd as much as admitted he'd be no threat to Sinclair if he attacked…The more he thought about it, the more it made sense. The bastard had set him up. He'd never wanted him as an ally. He'd only wanted confirmation that he would not be stopped.

"Dinnae go. I'm begging ye to stay with me. I'll

marry ye. We'll have our own bairns."

"I can't. I will not marry a man I don't respect." She twirled around and ran toward the pool. "I thought I loved you, Brann," she called over her shoulder, "but I was wrong. I was so wrong that you've torn my heart in two and stomped on it."

She finally came to the edge of the pool, and he couldn't do anything more than watch as she lifted her woolen gown over her head. She stood in front of him with naught on but her chemise, her beauty nearly taking his breath away. Climbing onto a rock, she dipped her feet into the water. Then she stepped into it, moving away from the side so she could dip her shoulders underneath the surface.

And he was in shock as he watched her hold her breath and dip down into the water.

CHAPTER TWENTY-TWO

ALLIE SPUN AROUND TO TAKE one last look at her gorgeous Highlander, at this person who'd made her feel both wanted and needed. She had two purposes here: to love and cherish him and act as a caregiver to his entire clan.

Her mind was made up. Even though she had no idea if this would even work, she had to try. So furious with the stubborn man, she wanted more than anything to be reunited with her sisters. She held her breath and dropped to her knees in the water, hoping the magic would take hold.

"Nay!" Brann's voice carried through the water as he grabbed her arm, pulling her back up out of the pool. He had to fall to his knees in order to reach her.

Her head nearly underwater, he pulled her back up and she yelled at him. "Let me go!"

"Nay, I'll no' let ye go. Ever. Can ye no' see we're meant for each other?"

"No. I can't love a man who would turn his head while his brother's clan is massacred."

She was close enough to see his jaw clench in frustration, but his grip didn't loosen and his eyes looked plaintive and remorseful. He meant what he said. His next words couldn't have surprised her more.

"I'll go. Just promise me ye willnae."

She stared at him, wondering if he was being truthful. "You will? You'll help your brother?"

"Aye, I'll help my brother. I'll swallow my foolish pride and go to him. For ye, if ye promise me ye'll stay."

"And you'll forgive him?" She'd never wanted to believe anyone more. It had taken all of her strength to close her eyes and drop to her knees. She didn't want to leave him.

"I'll forgive him. I promise. Now will ye promise me ye'll not go back? That ye'll marry me?"

"Will you help me look for my sisters? I know it's a long shot, and they're probably not even here, but I won't forgive myself if I don't keep looking."

He heaved a sigh. "God's bones, lass. I'm on my knees in front of ye, trying to keep a grip on ye so ye willnae disappear on me. I've said I love ye. I've asked ye to marry me. Can ye no' see I mean what I say? That I'd do whatever ye ask of me?" He lifted her out of the water with a roar and sat down on a huge boulder, settling her on his lap. "Aye, I'll marry ye, help ye look for yer sisters, and forgive my brother. I'll go to assist him myself. Shite, but ye're a demanding woman."

She smiled and cupped his face. "I love you, and I'll stay. Did you mean it when you said you loved me?"

"Ye need to ask me that? Would I have followed

ye here? Would I have changed my entire world around if I didn't? Woman, must I say it again?"

She snickered and nodded her head. "Yes."

"As ye wish. I love ye, Allison Sutton, more than I ever thought possible. Ye make me daft, so it must be love. Will ye marry me?"

"Yes…aye…absolutely."

He kissed her and she sighed because she loved the taste of this man so much.

"Come. I'm starting to have a bad feeling about my brother. We have nae time to waste. Don yer gown and let's go."

He helped her dress and lifted her onto her horse. She was grateful it was a warm day, or she would have been freezing in her damp clothes.

He led the way, setting a fast pace, but stopped outside his keep and said to Angus, "Gather me a hundred men of the two hundred ye have. Leave the rest to protect the castle. Have ye heard anything about Taran?"

"Only that he's under attack."

"We're going to assist him. I'd have ye stay behind, Allison, but I think we may need ye. Just do yer best to stay out of the way when we get there."

They headed toward Taran's land, riding side by side at the front of the group of warriors, guards strategically placed around Allison.

Adrenaline coursed through Allie's system, and she found herself mentally reviewing everything that had happened to bring them here. Their conversation at the pool. Lachie's sickness. The events at the festival…the festival. Something strange stood out to her. Something she should have recalled before now.

The man who'd taken her captive had said only one word. Shit.

Only one word, yes, but it was a telling word. She'd definitely heard it as shit, not shite. People from medieval times said shite. Was it possible? Her thoughts were foolish, so she shook her head to clear them away.

But there was no time to dwell on it. They arrived on Taran's land, and it was a bloody battlefield. She'd never seen so many dead in one area. Some men were sliced clear across their bellies, their intestines visible, their eyes dull and staring at the sky. Some bodies had an arrow protruding from their hearts, from their necks. Anywhere.

Brann's face was twisted with guilt, but fury and determination quickly overtook those other emotions, transforming him once more into the fierce Highlander the others rightfully feared. Brann waved her back.

"Do not go in the keep. They may have already taken it. Find a set of trees off to the side and stay hidden. I'll find ye when this is over."

Allie didn't hesitate to get out of the way. She'd never seen anything so horrifying.

Saying a quick prayer for the massacre to stop, she found what she thought would be a safe area in a copse of trees, well hidden from the melee of warriors.

She turned around to take one last look at the battlefield, hoping to see Brann. She found him up near the front of the battlefield. Taran was there, too! And, thank God, the MacKay plaids now outnumbered the enemy. The other plaids were mostly Sinclair plaids. Just as they'd suspected.

That was her last thought before she was taken. A random horse came galloping out of the woods, and the rider grabbed her around the waist, tossed her over his horse, and took off back toward the woods.

Brann would have absolutely no idea where she'd gone.

Brann unsheathed his sword and let out the MacKay warrior whoop as he made his way toward the front of the battlefield, cutting down any man who stood in his way.

As soon as he made it to the battle line where defender met attacker, he searched the area for his brother and finally found him fighting front and center ahead of his men. Despite the number of dead, the warriors who still stood fought hard, evidence of their good training. When Taran dispensed with the Sinclair fool in front of him, he met Brann's gaze and nodded. The numbers were now in their favor. The massacre would end.

Brann thrust himself into the battle, swinging his sword with a fierceness he hadn't possessed in a long time. He didn't wish to admit the reason why, but truth be told, his brother looked fatigued.

Three men came at Brann, and he turned his horse just a touch to give himself room to swing a wide arc with his blade, cutting one man across the belly and a second one across his chest with the same swing. He took the third one out with a flat-bladed blow that knocked him to the ground, after which his own comrade's horse trampled him.

Then something Brann had always dreaded happened right in front of him. He turned back to his brother and watched as someone cut Taran down, slicing his side. He lost his grip on his sword and fell off his horse, and two of his men quickly fell in around him.

Brann launched himself at the enemy with a fury he hadn't known he possessed. He and his men made quick work of the remaining enemy force before the last few still on horseback retreated off the field. He might have chased after the bastards, but he needed to tend to his brother first.

What a fool he'd been. Allison had been exactly right. He shuddered to think of what could have happened had he not listened to her. This was where he belonged—protecting his brother. Though skilled compared to most warriors, Taran did not have Brann's natural abilities.

Yet he'd still fought in the front line, defending his castle as any chieftain should. Brann was proud of him. Reaching Taran, he jumped off his horse and dropped down to his side, barking instructions at the two guards near Taran. His brother's eyes were closed, and fear nearly choked him.

He set his hand on Taran's shoulder and called to him. He didn't move. Blood had drenched his tunic and began to pool beneath him.

Pressure, that was what Allison and his mother had always said was best for a wound. He ripped his tunic apart to give him better access to the wound just as two of his men joined him.

"Angus," he bellowed as he pressed down on Taran's wound. "Find Allison. My brother needs her."

Taran's eyes opened and he caught Brann's gaze. Relief almost choked him. "Many thanks to ye, Brann. 'Tis over?"

"Aye, we finished them. A handful retreated on their own, the bastards. I should have been here sooner. My apologies."

"Nay." Taran reached for his hand. "I hurt ye, but I hoped ye'd heal with time. I knew ye had nae feelings for her, but I went about it the wrong way. Ye were right to be angry with me. But I'm grateful for my clan that ye came to our aid."

"Sinclair's men did this. Did ye see any other plaids?"

"Aye, Sinclair and some others I did no' know. Mayhap reivers he hired."

"Save yer breath, Taran."

"Nay, tell Shona I love her." His lids fluttered closed. "I fear I may no'…"

"Taran. Wake yer lazy arse up. Ye'll no' be leaving when I've just found my way back. Lachie needs ye, Taran. And so do I. Allison is my betrothed and I want ye at our wedding."

His brother opened his eyes long enough to give him a brief smile. "I'm happy for ye…Tell Shona. Dinnae forget…"

"Ye'll no' die. Allison will fix ye up as soon as she gets here."

Taran closed his eyes and his hand dropped to his side.

Angus's voice called out to him. "Chief, there's a problem."

Brann looked up at his second, hoping to see Allison at his side, but he was alone.

"Her horse is there, but she's missing, I cannae find her anywhere."

CHAPTER TWENTY-THREE

ALLIE FOUGHT THE BRUTE WITH all her might, kicking, screaming, and scratching everywhere. Then she noticed something.

The man had a tattoo on his hand, and his arm showed signs of recent scratches, now healing.

"Stop. I promise not to hurt you," he said. "Shit, you don't give up, do you? You're like a bearcat."

He stopped his horse and Allie forced herself to sit up so she could look him square in the eye.

"Where did you come from? There are no bear-cats in Scotland."

"My mother," he drawled, dismounting before he helped her down. "Isn't that the usual joke from back in our time?"

He had light brown hair, brown eyes, and a full beard that made him look older than he probably was. Most of all, he look tired and something else—defeated. That was it.

"Our time? What do you mean our time?" She couldn't believe how fast her heart beat as she waited for his answer. Had she been right about him?

"The twenty-first century. Planes, cars, cell phones, toilets, showers. You remember all of those things, don't you?" He waved her over to a nearby log, where they both sat down. "I'm not out to hurt you. I'm sorry if I did when I dropped you from my horse. That chieftain of yours is too powerful, too fast. I can't get slaughtered in medieval Scotland—my wife and family need me. I just want to talk to you. I need to get back."

"Okay, from the beginning. Who are you, and how and when did you get here?" Hope suddenly blossomed inside her. This man understood exactly what she'd gone through, and maybe he could even tell her what had become of her sisters.

But did she still wish to go back? No, she didn't, but if her sisters were here, she needed to find them. She had to find out what he knew.

"My name is Sam Billings. I'm from present-day Scotland. I happened to stop at Leannan Falls at about the same time as you and your sisters. I live not far from there, and I like to hike there every so often. I don't know what possessed me to stop that day, but when I listened to you three trying to convince each other to jump over the edge, I couldn't help but watch."

"You saw us jump?" Her hands began to tremble because she knew exactly what this could mean.

"Aye. I saw the three of you jump, and I walked over to the edge to make sure you all came up, but there was a problem. You didn't."

"Did my sisters come up for air?" Her voice came out in a whisper. She closed her eyes, waiting for his answer.

"Nay. That's why I'm here. None of you came up. All three of you jumped in and disappeared. I thought you were drowning, so I dialed the police to report it, but then I jumped in after you. I came up in a different waterfall. I was alone and it wasn't modern times anymore."

"Then you don't know where my sisters are?"

"Nay. But they didn't come up either, so they must be here somewhere. I'm sorry to have scared you, but I need to go back. I have a wife and a daughter. Can you help me? Did you know this would happen to the three of you?"

Allie reached for his hands, saddened that this man had come through with them because of their foolishness, hopeful that this meant her sisters truly had traveled in time with her. "No, I had no idea this would happen. I don't know how to get back, but we can work together. How did you find me? Are you the one who tried to grab me at the festival?"

"Aye. And at the MacKay Castle. When I first got here, I wandered around until I found people, and I ended up on Sinclair land. He accepted me as a warrior. I had to learn to handle a frickin' sword that's bigger than I am, but at least I do go to my gym regularly at home. I went back to the pool and tried to reverse it, but it didn't work. Sinclair promised to help me if I could find a way to diminish the MacKay and Murray numbers, so I poisoned the casks of ale."

"*You* did it? What did you use?"

He shrugged, looking chagrined. "I'm a biologist working in infection control. You do no' want to know what I did. It shouldn't have killed anyone, but it would have weakened them all considerably. I'm not proud, but I was desperate at the time. Have you tried to go back?"

"Yes. I tried to submerge myself in the pond where I landed after the jump. There was no swirling of energy, nothing unusual like the first time. Brann had a grip on me, but I don't think it would have worked."

"Have you heard anything about Leannan Falls? I have no way of knowing how far we are from it, but I'd like to go back. There's some sort of legend about the falls."

The odd woman at the festival had told her that "he" was searching for her. Surely, she'd meant Sam. Did that mean the rest of her advice should be followed?

"I didn't think much of it at the time," she said, "but I met a strange woman at the festival. She told me that a man was looking for me, and she also implied I should go to Edinburgh. That's close to the falls. Maybe we'll find a way for you to go home."

Sam immediately perked up. "Wow, do you think she was really a seer?"

"No. Maybe. I don't know what I believe. Common sense tells me she had no idea who I was when I spoke with her, but common sense also says there's no such thing as time travel. I still wake up every day wondering what I'm doing in medieval Scotland."

"Will you go to Edinburgh with me? Maybe you have special powers or something and I just got sucked in by your energy."

"I have to talk to Brann, but I promise to do

what I can if you'll help me search for my sisters."

He held his hand out for a shake. "Deal."

She stood and then glanced at his attire. "You better ditch that Sinclair plaid first."

Brann was sick with worry. Where could she have gone? "Taran, I'll find Allison after I get ye back to yer keep. She can sew ye up. Ye know how strong her skills are." He lifted his brother up as gingerly as he could. They weren't far from the keep, so he strode through the gates and toward the steps. He was almost at the door when Shona flung it open.

Taran had closed his eyes again, and Shona shrieked at the sight of him.

"Shona, go back inside and put some plaids on yer longest trestle table," Brann said. "I'll set him down so Allison can sew him. Ye can clean him up a bit, have someone help ye, and give him cool water that's been boiled for at least five minutes."

She nodded, sobbing so desperately he felt a tinge of sorrow for her. Somehow, she found the composure to summon a maid, and they set up a trestle table. Brann set his brother down and turned to the door.

"Ye're leaving?" Shona asked. "Are there more to attack us?"

"Nay. I'll leave a few men on the steps and several at the gates. I have to find Allison."

He spun on his heel, charged out the door, and raced down the steps. As soon as he mounted, he yelled to Angus.

"Ride along with me and tell me what ye've

learned."

"A man on horseback came for her and charged back into the woods. We can follow their path." Angus pointed in the direction they'd gone, and moments later they were in fast pursuit.

Brann had never felt so lost. Lachie was sick, Taran was near death's door, and Allison was missing. What had happened? He'd been happy as hell for about an hour after he'd convinced Allison to stay.

They hadn't gone far when they saw a horse grazing not far ahead. He motioned for Angus to slow his horse, but he couldn't afford to be strategic. Taran was dying.

To his surprise, he found her sitting on a log chatting with a man.

"I'll kill ye, ye bastard!" He jumped off his horse, but Allison bounded off the log and stood in front of him. The only reason he didn't thrust the end of his sword through the swine's black heart was the look on Allison's face. There was no fear there at all, something that made him hesitate.

"No, Brann. It's all right. He's from my land."

Brann turned to Angus and said, "Check the rest of the area for any other Sinclairs." Once his second was out of hearing range, he nodded at Allison. "Give me a good reason why I don't skewer his belly instantly, and ye best be quick about it."

"Please listen for a moment before you act. This is important to me."

"Ye know him?"

"No." Her shoulders fell. "He saw the three of us jump into the water and thought we were drowning when we didn't surface, so he jumped in after us. He came through the portal but landed in a different place."

"I don't want your woman. I'm married, but I do need her help to get back. I have a wife and daughter back home."

Brann said, "We can discuss this later. Allison, Taran took a sword to his side and he needs stitching. If ye dinnae come now, I fear he could die. He's losing a lot of blood."

"Badly hurt, Brann? Is he able to speak with you?"

"Barely. We need to hurry."

She nodded, quickly moving to his side. "I'll come now. Sam, follow us back. We'll talk later. Brann, have you another plaid he can wear?"

Brann tossed him one from his saddlebag, then lifted Allison and set her in front of him. He was already galloping back to the keep when he said, "Seems ye were right, lass. I'll no' be able to bear it if I lose my brother from my own foolishness."

"Please do all ye can to save him."

Allie rubbed her hands together to keep them from shaking.

"Ye can fix him, lass?"

"Brann, I'm not a doctor. I'll do my best, but I've never stitched anyone before."

"But ye know how to do it. Ye know what his insides are like, where to sew, do ye no'?"

"Yes. I'll see what I can do." How she prayed the Lord would give her guidance to save him. Brann would never forgive her if anything happened.

As if he read her mind, he said, "If he doesnae make it, 'twill no' be yer fault, lass. I should have been here sooner. If I had, I could have prevented it. And if ye had no' convinced me to come, he and his men would probably all be dead. Ye have my undying gratitude for that. The situation was far worse than I expected. What the hell was I thinking?"

"What matters is what you do from now on. Forget the past."

Once they reached the stables, he helped her down. He grabbed her hand, but instead of immediately ushering her inside, he tugged her close and kissed her forehead. "I do love ye, Allison."

She grinned at the sound of her name with the Scottish accent. Why did that one comment make her heart sing?

She hurried up the courtyard and into the great hall, where she washed her hands with the hand sanitizer she always carried with her. She did a quick assessment, pleased to see the wound hadn't damaged any internal organs, then instructed Shona and her maid as to what she would need.

After Shona left to do her bidding, Taran opened his eyes and said, "After ye finish, I wish for ye to ask Shona for my mother's box. 'Tis well hidden and she is the only one who knows where 'tis."

"Mama's box? What are ye talking about, Taran? Ye're no' dying, so stop being so morbid."

"And stop bossing me around like ye used to do when we were younger, Brann." He managed a small grin. "But 'tis good to hear yer voice, even if yer words do vex me. Mama gave me this box before she died, and she gave me strict instructions that I was never to give it to ye or Lachie."

"Why?" Brann fell onto a nearby stool.

His brother took a moment before he answered. "Mama made me memorize her words, though I dinnae understand them at the time. She said she came through the faerie pool, fell in love with Da, and decided to stay. She also said another would be coming, but she knew no' if she would be for ye or Lachie. She said I would know when the time came, and that if I met the lassie, I should give her the box. I know no' what is in there. 'Tis sealed."

Allison couldn't have been more stunned. She stumbled and Brann jumped up to catch her and set her upright. "Ye are hale?"

"Yes, I just…"

How did she know?

But it was no time to ask. Taran needed treatment now, so she set to work as soon as Shona brought her tools for her. Though she had none of the modern tools a doctor from her time would use, she washed his wound free of debris and then placed careful stitches after giving him ale to help with the pain. Twenty-first century Sam came in at some point and quickly moved over toward the hearth, his color a little green.

An hour later, she finished, pleased with her work, so she sent Brann home to grab her bag of treasures out of the chest. She could at least give the man a naproxen for his pain.

Taran fell asleep after drinking enough water to satisfy her. With Brann gone, she turned to Shona and said, "I'd like to see Taran's mother's box."

Shona nodded. "He told me he wished for ye to have it. Follow me. 'Tis in our chamber."

Once she pulled it out of the chest, Shona said, "Ye are welcome to look at it here alone. I'll not bother ye. Thank ye for saving my husband." She swiped at the tears flowing down her cheeks.

Allie wished she could tell her not to worry, but the risk of infection was huge. "He's not healed yet, and he may get an infection…"

"A what?"

"A fever. He could still get the fever." Wasn't that what they called an infection? "We'll all say our prayers that he will not."

Shona smiled through her tears and left, closing the door behind her.

Allie opened the box and gasped.

CHAPTER TWENTY-FOUR

ALLIE SET THE BOX DOWN and gingerly pulled out the contents. Inside was a lighter, a pair of plastic gloves, and a name tag that said, "Gwyndolyn Loudon, RN." She held the name tag in her hands, brushing her fingers across the blue, embossed, raised letters. Peeking back inside the box, she also found three syringes. She lifted the first one out and held it up to the light from the window. The needle was intact, and the cap was still in place. It was an older glass syringe, so if she had to guess, the woman was from a slightly earlier time than her. Syringes were syringes and had been in use for decades, though they'd become more disposable over the years. If she needed to use her vial of penicillin on Taran, she could.

Carefully, she set those aside and picked up an envelope made out to "The next Mrs. MacKay." She opened it, wondering what would be inside, and was surprised to see a handwritten letter on the strangest paper she'd ever seen.

My dear,

If you are reading this, then you have come through the portal to this wonderful area of the Highlands I now call home. Yes, I was a nurse living in Scotland in the 1960s, running myself ragged trying to care for sick people in a hospital, not taking care of myself, and living a very unhappy life.

If this sounds familiar, then you've come to the right place.

The odd fact is I didn't realize how unhappy I was until I fell through the portal and met my husband.

And now? Life is wonderful. Three strong sons and a sweet husband who loves me and protects me as if I'm the most treasured jewel of all.

You'll have to give up hot showers, telephones, and chocolate, but it was worth it for me, and something tells me the same may be true for you. I know you're a nurse, like I am, and your skills will be desperately needed here. There will be struggles, for sure, but you'll find the work far more rewarding than bedpans and morphine, and you won't have anyone telling you what to do.

I don't know why I am so sure you'll be coming, but I am. I met you in a dream.

Love my son and become a caregiver unlike any other. You are so needed here.

Please stay.

But if you feel you cannot, in order to return, you must go to Leannan Falls south of Edinburgh. You'll need to meet the seer first. It's the only way.

But also understand this—if it's not in your heart to return, you will not.

Until we meet someday,

Gwyndolyn Loudon MacKay RN

Tears ran down her cheeks, but they were tears of joy. Oh, how she loved Brann MacKay. She'd had to travel thousands of miles and hundreds of years to find her true home.

Gwyndolyn MacKay had put her decision into words she could understand.

She was needed here.

Her life at home had revolved around her parents, and when they'd died, a little piece of her had died with them.

Twenty-first-century Allison no longer had a purpose.

Here she was loved and admired, and yes, *needed*.

The tears sliding down her cheeks slowed, and she started when she noticed Brann standing in the doorway watching her.

"Are ye all right? Did ye find anything surprising?"

She chuckled, swiping at her tears. "A letter from your mother. She said she dreamed about me. She asked me to stay."

"And what else?"

"I'll tell you the rest later. It isn't important. Just know that her words spoke to me and they couldn't have come at a more perfect time."

"And ye're staying?"

Poor Brann. She couldn't imagine how he felt, knowing the woman he loved could choose to walk away from him, never to be seen again. The hopefulness in his gaze and his voice told her how much he cared for her. She stood and moved over to stand in front of him, wrapping her arms around his neck.

"Aye, I'm staying."

While Allie tended Taran, Brann had gone to the Murray hold to make sure all was well. He'd discovered that Sinclair had been killed during that skirmish.

Allie knew Brann wished he'd been the one to kill the bastard, but at least justice had been served. She didn't even say "I told you so" when he admitted that Murray had thanked him profusely, saying they never would have defeated Sinclair without Brann's warriors.

She and Brann had agreed to bring Sam to Leannan Falls in Edinburgh after Taran's health improved. Perhaps they would find her sisters there, too, although she didn't dare say so out loud. But first they had to wait.

Taran ended up with a roaring infection, so Allie gave him one injection of penicillin, but he was up and moving again after another few days. It was time to leave. She gave Shona thorough instructions on changing his bandages, and they headed out with Sam. Brann had sent Angus back to his castle to bring Lachie over to sit with their brother.

Their next stop would be Edinburgh. Allie had shared some of the contents of Gwyndolyn's letter, and it had given Sam a spark of hope, especially given what the seer had told Allie at the festival.

"Ye must go to Leannan Falls," Shona had said. "Ye should always listen to the wisdom of yer elders."

Allie had spent some time getting to know Shona, and she'd managed to rope Brann into a few of the conversations. They were kin, so she felt it important to help the two put their past behind them. She did not want their issues to continue interfering with the brothers' relationship.

Once they arrived in Edinburgh, they found an inn and settled in for a midday meal. They agreed to look for another seer at the merchants' booths in the center of town. Hopefully, she would be able to direct them to the falls.

Brann had insisted on bringing a dozen guards, though the threat of Allie being taken captive had diminished now that Sam had admitted to his part in it.

Brann led the way into the vendors' area, stopping to ask questions at each booth. "Have ye heard of any seers here?"

At about the sixth booth, he finally got an answer. "She's over yonder. The old woman travels quickly. She willnae stay long, but she seems to be awaiting something or someone."

Allie spun her head around and found her instantly.

It was the same woman she'd seen at the festival.

Allie decided to call her out on her fib. "I thought you said you weren't a seer."

The old woman fussed with the gray strands that had escaped her plait, a wide grin on her face. "I wasn't a seer there. Only in Edinburgh. They cannot handle a seer in such a small area. I prefer to remain a mystery. 'Tis the way of magic in Scotland. Ye are in special need of my assistance, but ye must promise no' to reveal my secrets or I'll no' help ye." She winked, something that caused Allie to notice why her gaze was so odd. She had one blue eye and one green.

Sam just stared at her, giving Allie a nudge. "Agreed," he whispered.

Allie nodded, then said, "We need your help, so I'll agree to keep your identity a secret."

"Good," she said, her eyes sparkling. "I see ye've met the person who was looking for ye." She crossed her arms, taking Sam's measure. "Ye need to get back. Whoever ye are, ye were no' meant to be here. 'Twas an accident that ye fell through."

He glanced at Allie, who gave him a nod of hope, then turned back to the seer. "Just tell me how. I'm eager to get back to my family."

She looked at Allie and said, "Take him to Leannan Falls. If he's the only one in the water and he drops beneath the surface, he'll go back."

"Just like that?" Sam asked.

"Take this stone with ye just to be sure." She reached into a small box and pulled out a stone, placing it in the palm of his hand. Small, clear, and polished, it nearly glowed in the sunlight. "Dinnae lose it." She winked at him and moved over to talk to another customer.

Allie asked Brann, "Do you know where Leannan Falls is?"

"Nay. I'll get directions from her when she's finished."

She squeezed Brann's hand, then waited for the woman to finish. She hadn't even had the opportunity to ask about her sisters.

The woman sensed their purpose, so she spoke directly to Brann. "Head south, 'tis straight south for half of the hour, then follow the crooked path to the east. Ye'll no' miss it."

She spun away from her before Allie could ask her important question, dismissing them with her hand.

She was tempted to wait her out, but Sam gave her an imploring look. The poor man was impatient to get back to his loved ones. They'd return once he was safely on his way home.

They headed back to where they'd left their horses, but a voice called to her from behind. "Allison Sutton?"

She spun around at the mention of her full name, praying one of her sisters had called to her, but in her heart she knew it wasn't so. The voice wasn't familiar. To her surprise, the seer was the one who'd spoken.

As Allie stared at her, waiting for her to explain, all the sounds at the festival diminished so that there were only two people there, as far as she was concerned. Allie and the seer, who said to her, "After he's gone, come back to see me. Ye *do* belong here, and yer journey is no' finished."

Allie raced back to the woman and whispered, "My sisters?"

The woman shook her head and closed her eyes. "Send him back first."

CHAPTER TWENTY-FIVE

THEY ARRIVED AT LEANNAN FALLS a short time later, pleased to find no one else in the area. Brann helped her dismount and she raced over to the edge, staring up at the top of the falls in wonder. The emotion roiling in his gut was more akin to fear.

"That's it. This is the one we came through," Allison declared, her head tipped back to take in the top of the waterfall.

"Do you think I need to jump in the way we did before?" he asked Allison.

"No," she replied. "With that stone in your hand, I think it won't matter. Go to the middle of the pool and duck under. If it doesn't work, you can always climb to the top and jump."

Sam's smile stretched from ear to ear. "Good idea," he said. "My apologies, but I'm no' waiting. Thank you both for your help, but I'm in a hurry to get home. I wish you luck."

Without saying another word, he climbed into the water and trudged through the pool until he was in the middle. Once the water was deep enough, he spun around to look at them one last time.

Brann moved over to her side and grasped her hand, intertwining their fingers. She held his hand with a death grip as though she still feared the seer was wrong.

Sam held the stone up for them to see, then dipped his head under the water.

Just like that, he was gone.

Allison giggled, turning to Brann and saying, "It worked. I think it really worked."

Something landed at the edge of the pool, nearly at her feet. Allison leaned down to pick it up from the water, surprised to see it was the stone the healer had given Sam.

She turned it over in her fingers, then held it up for Brann to see. "I think I'll save it."

Brann reached over to run his fingers through her wild waves, massaging the back of her neck. "Allie…"

Her gaze popped up to his. "You called me Allie, not Allison." A small smile crept across her face as their eyes met. His gaze then lowered to the small rock she tossed from one palm to the other. Did she wish to use it?

"If ye still feel the need, then go ahead and go back." Hell, but that was the most difficult statement he'd ever made in his life.

She frowned, confusion all over her face. "You don't want me to stay?" He could see the smallest amount of moisture welling in the corners of her eyes.

He cupped her cheek and kissed her lips, drawing out the moment so it would live in his memory. Finally, he said, "I dinnae want ye to ever leave me, but I wish for yer happiness more than anything. If ye must go back to be happy, then I want ye to go back."

Allison just stared at him, her jaw dropping open. Nothing came out for several moments, and he watched as various emotions crossed her features, her big heart and her quick mind driving her thoughts in multiple directions.

Love, confusion, sadness, regret, so many emotions appeared to cross her face.

"Allie, 'tis all right. If ye feel ye must go back, I'll understand." His thumb brushed her cheek before he brought it across her lower lip, now trembling. "Please dinnae cry. I can tolerate anything but that."

She gripped his hand and kissed his palm. "You do love me. Only a man who loves me would tell me to go back."

He glanced up at the gray clouds in the sky, saying a quick prayer that she'd choose him, but knowing he needed to let her go if she did not. "Aye, I do love ye."

She tossed the stone over her shoulder, and they both listened to it land with a resounding plop. Brann smiled and she threw her arms around his neck and said, "No. I'm staying here. I love you too much to leave you. No matter what happens with my sisters, I'll stay here with you. I wish to hold our bairns in my arms someday."

He buried his face in her neck and hugged her around the waist, hoping she wouldn't see the tears in his eyes. When had he ever been this happy?

She pushed back from him and said, "But I would

like to return to the seer. Maybe she knows something about my sisters. It makes sense that they came through also, but there's no way of knowing where they landed. Maybe one of them is here. Maybe…"

He kissed her, suckling on her bottom lip for a second before he said, "Back to Edinburgh we go."

They'd returned to the merchant's area in Edinburgh, but to Allie's dismay, the seer was no longer there. In tears, she searched every path, every road, and every tent. To no avail. The woman had disappeared.

"Come," Brann said. "We'll find an inn and spend the night here. Mayhap she'll return in the morn. 'Tis late."

Allie's heart was breaking, but she nodded and went along with him, simply because she had no other ideas. If the seer was gone, how could she ever find her sisters? She barely registered what was happening as Brann led her into an inn and made arrangements for their stay. They ate beef stew in the common room, then returned to their chamber. Allie glanced around the simple room, but she didn't really care what it looked like. She just wanted the night to end so she could begin her search again in the morning.

Not wishing to upset Brann, who looked almost as concerned as she felt, she said, "I'm a bit tired. Do you mind if I go to sleep early?"

He shook his head, kissed her quickly on the lips, and said, "I'm going to check on the horses. I dinnae always trust these places with my horse. Star is special."

She managed to nod, but as soon as he left, she fell onto the bed and let herself sob. Before she knew it, she was fast asleep.

Brann crept down the stairs, not knowing exactly what he was to do, but he had to try something. After watching Sam just disappear in front of them, it had struck him, hard, that Allison could have disappeared just as easily.

She truly was from the future, and yet she'd chosen to stay with him.

This beautiful, feisty lass from a far-off century had come into his world and saved both of his brothers, perhaps even part of his family's land, and she'd taught him how to love fully, holding nothing back.

He had to find her sisters. If they were truly in Edinburgh, he would find them. Fate had to be on their side.

A sudden image in his mind of his mother caught him. "Mama? Ye wanted me to accept her. Can ye no' help me find her sisters?" Daft, he was turning daft over a lass. He shook himself and whispered, "Just lead the way, Mama."

He wandered down the street until he reached another inn, which he entered. He glanced around the inn's dining hall for anything unusual, but nothing stood out to him. After asking the innkeeper to look out for two lasses who spoke with a strange accent, he continued on his way. The same search at two more taverns yielded the same lack of results, but he kept going, searching the streets as he went.

He started to lose hope. "Mama? I could use a wee bit of help here."

But what he saw at the fourth inn made him pause. Two young brown-haired lasses sat at a table, whispering furiously, while two men stood guard. At least, they appeared to be guarding the women.

Brann stepped inside the establishment and found a table not far from the group, ordering an ale from the serving lass, who gave him a saucy come-hither look that he ignored. He watched the two lasses, trying to overhear their talk to determine if they shared Allison's strange accent, until one of the guards moved closer to him. The man wore an unfamiliar plaid, but there was no mistaking the glare he gave Brann as he crossed his arms in front of his chest. "Stop yer staring. She belongs to me," he growled.

Brann did not recognize him, but he did notice something that almost caused him to yell so loudly it would have echoed off the farthest peak in the Highlands.

The two lasses had turned to him when the guard spoke, and their blue eyes were the same unusual shade as Allison's. What names had she called her sisters?

The Highlander reached for him just as he shouted, "Hannah and Caroline Sutton? I know where Allison is."

The two ladies leaped from their seats, one knocking the chair over from her exuberance. "Allie? You know where Allie is?"

Aye, there was no denying it. It was the same exact accent, the same eyes, the same hope he'd seen in Allie's gaze.

Allie thought she heard a sound at the door. Brann awakened her with a kiss a short time later, though it seemed like she'd slept three days away. It was still dark out, and he surprised her by holding his hand out to her and beckoning her out of the bed.

"What? Where are we going?"

"Just trust me. We willnae be long."

"Did you find the seer?"

"Nay," he whispered, not saying anything more, just squeezing her hand.

She sighed and followed him down the creaky staircase, hoping they weren't bothering anyone. The inn wasn't well lit so she clung to his shoulder as she followed him down the stairs and out the door.

The warm breeze hit her first. Medieval Scotland was a wonderful place, even in the dark of night. She rested her head on his shoulder, no longer caring where they were going.

She loved him and trusted him completely.

They strolled in the quiet of the night toward Edinburgh Castle. Brann tugged her to a stop when they reached a cobblestone courtyard lit up with torches, almost a park-like setting. Tucking her in close, he kissed the top of her head, then cupped her cheeks and said, "Remember that I love ye."

She had no idea what brought this on, but she

followed his lead as he turned her toward the center of the courtyard.

She saw nothing. Scowling, she turned back toward him to demand an explanation, but he just tipped his head and smiled at her.

A voice called out in the night. "Allie?"

Another voice echoed the first. "Allie, is it you?"

She *knew* those voices. She spun around, fearing all the while her senses deceived her. This was something she'd wanted so much she worried it was another dream.

Even in the dark, she recognized Caroline's lithe form running toward her, Hannah's voice coming from behind her. "Finally!"

She took off at a dead run toward her sisters, launching herself at the two of them with a squeal. Within seconds the three of them were jumping up and down like five-year-olds, hugging each other, crying, mumbling, and carrying on as though they'd never been apart.

She stopped, grabbed each sister by the hand, and turned back to Brann, just then realizing that he'd gone off to search for them while she'd slept, knowing full well he might yet lose her to them.

Their gazes locked together, and she smiled, trying to pour all her love into it. He smiled back at her, then said, "I couldn't watch you like that. What you did for me and Taran, I had to try to do the same for you."

Caroline said, "You're keeping him, right? He searched all over for us."

"He's gorgeous," Hannah said. "I can't believe each of us met someone here! I'm already married and Caroline will be soon. You're going to marry him and stay with us, right, Allie?"

Allie couldn't believe her ears. "Hannah, you're already married?"

"Yes," she pulled back from her sisters and waved to a man behind her. "Meet my husband, Tristan." A tall, handsome man came forward, nodding to her. In the excitement of the reunion with her sisters, she hadn't even noticed the two hulking men standing behind them.

Caroline wasn't to be outdone. "Meet my husband-to-be, Callum MacMoran." The brawny Highlander smiled at Allie.

"Greetings to you both." Then she glanced from one sister to the other and squealed. "I can't believe this!" She tugged Brann forward. "Yes, we're marrying. I guess you've already met him, but this is Brann MacKay, Chieftain of the MacKays."

Caroline said, "Callum is Laird of the MacMorans."

"And Tristan is Lord of Saxford Castle."

Brann's eyes widened. "How is he English when ye all came from Scotland?"

Callum bellowed out a laugh and clapped Tristan on the back. "True, he's English, but he's no' a bad English."

"How did you end up in England, Hannah?" Allie asked.

"I don't know. I woke up on the shore off Saxford Castle without any memory at all. Where did you land?"

"In a faerie pool on MacKay land. I walked until I found a bunch of men fighting Black Brann." She pointed her thumb toward him over her shoulder.

Callum let out a low whistle. "I've heard of yer

skills, Black Brann." He nodded with appreciation. "Also heard ye were bested by a lass. Was Allie the one?"

Brann pointed his finger back at her. "Aye, she kicked me in the bollocks."

The group broke into gales of laughter.

"Allie, I can't believe it," Hannah shouted.

"You never would have done that in Maine," Caroline managed to get out between chuckles.

"Wait until you hear the whole story."

"Oh yeah? I bet you weren't taken back to a medieval castle and locked up, just like a common criminal." Caroline crossed her arms and pursed her lips, shooting an aggrieved look at her betrothed.

"I dinnae *exactly* lock ye up. I just said ye could-nae leave. I thought ye belonged to my enemy."

Hannah pointed to Tristan. "Well, *he* wanted me to pretend to be a whore."

"Not quite the complete truth, lass. I can explain," Tristan muttered. Turning to Brann, he asked, "Did she truly kick you in the bollocks?"

"A wee lass like that?" Callum added with a chuckle. "No wonder word got all the way to here in Edinburgh."

Brann shrugged and nodded. "Dinnae look so innocent, ye two. Ye couldnae ignore the feisty travelers any more than I could."

"Feisty?" Caroline repeated with a dangerous edge to her voice.

Callum cast her a sly grin and said, "Ye were a fiery hellion. Sounds like yer sisters are the same way."

"I was not," Caroline's retort rang out over the others. But she had her arms around her betrothed, and her actions belied her words.

"Allie? You think she's feisty?" Hannah asked, staring at Brann in disbelief. "I never thought I'd hear anyone call her that."

Brann quirked his brow and turned to face Allison. "Something new, lass?"

Allie turned the brightest shade of red possible, but she didn't let the embarrassment silence her like she might have done at home. She wrapped her arms around Brann and squeezed him tight. "Aye, he's made me into a feisty lass, ye know. And I'm never going back. I'm madly in love with him. Wait until I tell you everything that happened."

Brann wrapped his arm around her and leaned down to whisper something in her ear. She snickered and said, "Go ahead and ask them."

The group became silent at once, anxious to hear his question.

Brann tipped his chin up and asked, "Does anyone have any more of those dick covers?

~ THE END ~

FALLING FOR THE

HIGHLANDER

BOOK ONE in the
ENCHANTED FALLS TRILOGY
By Emma Prince

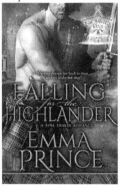

DESTINY THROWS HER BACK IN time. Can love make her stay?

Caroline Sutton doesn't belong here. Not in the Highlands, and certainly not in the fourteenth century. One minute, headstrong Caroline is standing at the edge of a waterfall, daring her two sisters to jump with her in hopes that it will make them all forget the recent death of their parents. The next minute, Caroline wakes up on the shores of a Highland loch—600 years in the past. She's determined to return to her sisters and her own time, but Callum, the rugged Highland Laird who discovers her, has other ideas. When heat flares between them, all Caroline's plans are thrown into jeopardy, but if she gives in to her blazing desire, she fears she may never want to leave the past behind.

Laird Callum MacMoran is in a bind. He has inherited a clan feud with no end in sight. When he comes across and strange and strikingly beautiful woman on enemy lands, he thinks to use her as a bargaining chip to end the bloodshed. Little does he know this odd lass is more than she seems, and falling for her will threaten the peace he has worked to build for so long. Torn between responsibility to his clan and his growing feelings for Caroline, can he love her enough to let her go? Or will fate decide their futures for them?

Get yours at Amazon.

FALLING FOR THE

KNIGHT

BOOK TWO in the
ENCHANTED FALLS TRILOGY
By Cecelia Mecca

HANNAH SUTTON PRIDES HERSELF ON
being a strong, independent woman, perfectly
in control of her career and personal life. But her
orderly existence is upended when she and her sisters travel to Scotland and jump off an enchanted
waterfall as a lark. After blacking out, she finds
herself marooned near a castle in England, alone.
Everyone she meets appears to be a devoted reen-
actor, dressed from head to toe in medieval gear,
but soon the truth becomes undeniable. Hannah
has traveled back in time.

Tristan wasn't meant to be a lord, but his bravery and prowess in battle earned him the lordship of Saxford. Now, he faces a challenge that might very well unseat him—his ten-year truce with Saxford's biggest enemy is about to come to an end. It's the worst possible time for a mysterious woman to wash up on his beach, especially one who claims to be from the future. But the beguiling beauty quickly gets under his skin, and he realizes there might be something to her claim.

Hannah and Tristan have an immediate attraction that grows deeper, and the longer she stays at Saxford, the more she begins to question if she wants to return to the future—or make a future with her medieval knight.

Get yours at Amazon.

ABOUT THE AUTHOR

KEIRA MONTCLAIR IS THE PEN name of an author who lives in Florida with her husband. She loves to write fast-paced, emotional romance, especially with children as secondary characters in her stories.

She has worked as a registered nurse in pediatrics and recovery room nursing. Teaching is another of her loves, and she has taught both high school mathematics and practical nursing.

Now she loves to spend her time writing, but there isn't enough time to write everything she wants! Her Highlander Clan Grant series, comprising of eight standalone novels, is a reader favorite. Her third series, The Highland Clan, set twenty years after the Clan Grant series, focuses on the Grant/Ramsay descendants. She also has a contemporary series set in The Finger Lakes of Western New York and a paranormal historical series, The Soulmate Chronicles.

Her latest series, The Band of Cousins, stems from The Highland Clan but is a stand-alone series.

Contact her through her website, *www.keiramontclair.com*.

Manufactured by Amazon.ca
Bolton, ON

13291062R00131